FROM SCRATCH: BOOK ONE
INHERITANCE

DENNIS HUFFINGTON

WWW.ENTERMEDIAONLINE.COM

Published by
Enter Media
2303 N 44th St. #14-1184
Phoenix, AZ 85008-2442

First Edition

ISBN: 978-0-9980125-1-3
Library of Congress Control Number: 2017900777

DEDICATION

To my 11-year old self.

You are awesome! Don't let anyone get you down!

TABLE OF CONTENTS

PREFACE

"Everyone's childhood plays itself out"

- Marilyn Monroe

The names in this book have been changed to protect the innocent. Me. I am the innocent.
Writing this book has been one of the most difficult things I've ever done. I've revisited some of the deepest and darkest places that I've ever been. The process has been mentally, emotionally, and even physically demanding. I would even say that some days were depressing. The life of this book has become a concrete representation of my trials and tribulations. There were many times that I didn't want to finish but I felt that if I succumbed to writing the book, it was the same as succumbing to the events and experiences written within it.

Nothing about it was easy and it hurt like hell to be honest about my life. The truth more than hurts and it can be excruciatingly painful. I did the best I could to try and relay to you what it felt like to be me. This is a true story but if you know me it may be hard for you to believe it because I have become an expert at hiding, masking, and downplaying my pain.

Telling my story evoked pain, shame, anger, confusion and embarrassment. These are the roots of my existence as I have developed as a man with a foundation based in trauma. I have lived with this story all my life but kept it all a secret, thinking I would be safer if I hid my truth. I now realize that my truth is my weapon.

Many of us will not have what it takes to pull ourselves from out of what we inherit at birth. Some of us will not even have the mindset to recognize the inheritance that we have been given. I say "us" because all of us are affected by our circumstances at birth, good or bad. Everyone of us is born into this world and given a name, a path, and an inheritance. We receive everything that we are from our family and the blessings and curses from prior generations are bestowed upon an innocent child. That is why babies come out kicking and screaming in frustration. At that very moment, when they leave the safe and beautiful peace of the womb, they are burdened with all that came before them. They call it living, but for many of us, life is more about dying.

As we grow and continue to live, our experiences and possessions are accumulated and treasured. Titles, accomplishments and status become prized possessions of the living as they will be the legacy of us when we leave the Earth. These prized possessions are the evidence of a good name and a life well lived. More importantly, these possessions are evidence of how one played the game of life. Upon death, we leave these things to our children and their children and their children's children, and so on and so forth. All so that we may, in our own way, live on forever. Not everyone passes on prized possessions though, and some of us inherit things that serve us no benefit.

If you're lucky, you will inherit wealth, status, and possibly even happiness. If you're unlucky, you will inherit nothing. If you're like me, you will inherit rejection, abandonment, and endless questions. I was born into a life of constant confusion and internal strife from both sides of my family. As much as I worked to fill voids, right the wrongs, and troubleshoot my problems, they kept reappearing. I constantly questioned myself and even my creator. Why me? What am I doing wrong?

When I first started writing this book, it was titled *From Scratch*. The titling of the book proved to be prophetic. My goal was to educate readers about the laws of attraction and how the universe works in our favor. It was a new way of thinking for me at one point and I had to work to replace much of the way that I used to think, which was very negative. My new outlook on life and way of thinking empowered me to the point where I was ready to take on the world. That was how I ended up letting go of everything, to go forth toward my destiny. That was what I meant by starting from scratch. That was my original intention.

The narrative was going to chronicle my journey as I moved and started over professionally. *From Scratch* took on several meanings throughout the writing of this book. As I was writing, life continued to happen and I felt the need to tell a much different story. It became obvious that I was also on a journey to better myself, also seemingly from scratch. The life that was happening while I was writing *From Scratch* soon became a more important story to tell. At that moment, the entire book was rewritten, from scratch. What you are about to read is actually not what I originally intended to share with you, but the message is still just as powerful.

Thank You

CHAPTER ONE: INHERITANCE

The warm Arizona sun brought a welcoming warmth and much needed Vitamin D. This was where life would be better and a new chapter would begin. I was convinced that GOD was here and surrounded me in the mountains, the sunlight, and the warmth. Years ago, a fleeting thought of the Phoenix bird crossed my mind and I considered the idea of moving to the warm, desert city. The idea of a booming and growing city wrapped in the warmth of the sun intrigued me. My body became warm with the just the thought.

The myth of the bird mesmerized me as well. The idea of rebirth in the midst of fire was both destructive and beautiful at the same time. We all should have the power to start over, press reset, give ourselves another chance, and destroy the parts in us that we no longer desire. I have always had an affinity to the poetic and literary, and as a result I tend to romanticize events in my life. I find myself applying literary elements to my daily life and looking for symbolism. The Phoenix bird symbolized rebirth and the city symbolized a place where people went to be reborn, or rise from their ashes.

After 15 years of living in St. Louis, I felt stripped and the need to be rebuilt. I needed a rebirth. It wasn't the first time that I wanted to leave St. Louis. In fact, moving had been a priority for most of the time I was in St. Louis but fear and uncertainty always prevented me from taking the leap and leaving. I had started over once when I moved to St. Louis, and I was afraid of what it would be like to have to start all over, once again. Phoenix was just one of the places that I had tossed around the idea of moving to but never took it under serious consideration. Then, what seemed like all of a sudden, it was my new home.

I continually find myself amazed at the workings

of GOD and the universe. A thought that I had put into the universe so long ago had come to fruition, at a time when it was most befitting to my life. Moving to Phoenix would rebirth me from my own ashes in the same fashion as the mythical bird. The rebirth would come as a result of following my dreams and putting all of my efforts into being the person that I wanted to be and leave behind the person that I was. The new me would emerge from the ashes of the old me as a writer and creative force in the world.

In order for this to happen, I had to leave behind all that no longer served me a purpose. That meant that I had to leave behind my career as a teacher, and completely forget about trying to save the lives of children in poverty. I was going to save my own life and through my story, I could possibly save others. There was a lot that needed to change and my body physically reacted to the mental changes that were taking place.

The first weeks in Phoenix were physically demanding on my body and mind. I was completely exhausted and couldn't do much without being tired. It wasn't a bad thing though, my body was purging and I needed to rest. Leaving St. Louis meant leaving behind a work environment that was killing me, a city plagued by violence and unrest, and painful memories and life lessons that scarred me as a teenager and young adult. My entire mindset changed, the very moment I pulled my car off of my apartment lot and left St. Louis and my body followed my mind immediately thereafter. Whether I called it a resurgence, a renewal, or a rebirth, I was becoming a better me.

I wouldn’t just forget about everything that happened in St. Louis. All that I had experienced would not be in vain. I decided that I was going to write a magnum opus covering all the chapters of my life. Living in St. Louis was going to be a major chapter. It was where I came into my own and learned how the world *really* works.

St. Louis is one of America's most historically relevant cities, but it has been plagued with a concentration of all of the problems that face America. As it continues to fall from its position as one of America's anchors, the people there have developed a tenacity and pride that resonates above all of the turmoil. It was complete culture shock moving there, living there, and seeing the impact the city has on those who live there. Writing a book about my experiences coming of age in St. Louis was going to be a guaranteed page turner.

It was never my choice to move to St. Louis. Of course we always have a choice in the sense of being able to make decisions for ourselves but when you have nowhere else to go, you typically choose food and shelter. I ended up there because I had nowhere else to go. If I knew then what I know now, I would've taken my chances elsewhere. I don't say that to knock the city or my experiences. I simply mean that I am a man of faith and not of fear at this point in my life. I have learned that what your life is at any given moment is what it should be at the time. You have to grasp your presence and recognize all the possibilities of your current situation.

I arrived in St. Louis at the tender age of 17, with a deficit in self-esteem, that continued to depreciate my self value. At 17, I knew nothing about the power of faith and favor or how my life could change based on the thoughts that I kept. Before I moved there, I was sleeping on my best friend's floor, after being put out of my grandmother's house. Nothing about life seemed to be going in my favor, and I was very negative about everything. Moving to St. Louis was the first time I would face the fire and rise from my own ashes.

In the years that followed, I worked extremely hard to pull myself out of poverty, and the toxic mental state that poverty puts us in. I went to college and graduate school while working to take care of myself. While I grew to be a strong young man there, I also evolved into someone jaded and pessimistic. In the process, I completely gave up on my dream of being a journalist. Journalism was a dream, and I needed a job and a career that would guarantee that I could provide for myself. I didn't have time to chase after dreams. Instead, I had nightmares. Nightmares about my childhood and upbringing, that recurred, and kept me from truly resting during my sleep.

Marilyn Monroe wrote in her diary, *Everyone's childhood plays itself out*. Hers apparently played out in her relationships and drug overdose. I pray that my childhood has already played itself out. During those first years in St. Louis, my childhood played out in my nightmares and haunted me in my waking life. Children have the most vulnerable spirits. When left with unfinished business, like all other spirits, those childhood spirits become ghosts and can haunt us well into adulthood.

Many of us find ourselves haunted by the ghosts of of our childhood. When we are born, we have no control as to what we are born into. As we struggle to overcome the lives that are handed to us at the time of our birth, we end up with unfinished business, leaving that childhood spirit to haunt us until we properly finish said business.

I had plenty of ghosts that haunted me, causing me to fear and fail on a regular basis. I was haunted by feelings of rejection, lack of love, and self-hatred. As a boy, I was very different than the others around me. Of course I didn't know I was different until I was told. The ways in which I was told were crushing to my childhood spirit and the pain it caused stayed with me. I found out that I was gay from others around me, through gay slurs, hate language, physical attacks, and harassment on a daily basis, no exaggeration.

My father obsessed over homosexuality and his idea of masculinity. He wouldn't even touch me, let alone hug me. I would watch him play with my cousins, who were girls, whenever they visited but he never played with me and I lived with him. He believed that any sort of male-to-male interaction would make him less than a man and would cause me to grow up to be homosexual. In his eyes, affection and love between men was a not masculine attribute. As a boy, I wasn't equipped to discern the difference between affection and love. The absence of affection felt like an absence of love to me. As I got older, I witnessed other fathers having no problem giving affection to their sons and all of their sons grew up to be normal. My theory is that had I received the proper affection from my father, I may have not sought love from other males. Maybe I would have turned out normal too.

My father followed a particular set of rules when it came to masculinity. If you didn't fall in line or act according to his rules, you were not a man. Men do not eat ice cream, fruit, or drink cappuccino. Men do not like to read books or appreciate art. Men do not play the flute or talk on the telephone. I'm not sure where the set of rules originated from but he was a stickler to them. He lived by these rules as if they had been both medically and scientifically proven and ordained in every religion known to man.

I can only imagine the complete and utter soul-shattering disappointment he must have felt when I began expressing feminine ways at a very young age. Everything that he focused his entire parenting style and existence on had been for naught. His worst nightmare, having a gay son, manifested before his very eyes, even as he did everything within his power to prevent it. Surely, he must have resigned to the idea that the universe was working against him. When combined with his other life experiences, it most certainly must have seemed that way to him.

I never understood why I was gay and I tried many

times to retrace the steps back in my life to where it may have first manifested within me. Of course, my father's family blamed in on my mother, as if I had inherited it from her. If only he had been exposed to the law of attraction at some point in his life. He focused his entire existence, his entire energy, on not having a gay son and being masculine. In return, he received from the universe what he focused on the most, a gay son. The law of attraction granted him what he focused on the most, whether he focused on what he wanted or what he didn't want.

Every day that passed, I vowed to leave the small town that I grew up in and never return. That was exactly what happened but not exactly as I had expected it. I viewed education as my only chance to move up in the world, at least that's what we were told growing up. My father and grandmother laughed in my face when I told them that I planned to go to college. They didn't believe that I was good enough for college. That didn't stop me though, it only motivated me more. I applied for schools in Atlanta and Baltimore, and got accepted to three. I was determined to make something of myself but an even stronger factor driving me was that my family didn't support me and had went as far as to ridicule me. I would show them.

My plans after high school were to attend Morgan State University in Baltimore and become a famous journalist. Specifically, I wanted to be the head anchor for *The Today Show*, since Bryant Gumbel had moved on. For my entire senior year, I mentally prepared myself for leaving home that summer. I made sure that I stayed on top of everything that I needed to do for school, from filling out applications, financial aid papers, and applying for housing. After graduating in June of 2001, it was time to make my final arrangements, which included securing housing on-campus.

My father and I had a major blowup fight because

he refused to give me money that I needed for the housing deposit. What made matters even worse is that I was given plenty of money to cover the housing deposit as graduation gifts when I graduated from high school. The money that I received directly, I put to use immediately, paying for various fees that my school required. The housing deposit was $500 and my Aunt Irene had put together a package with her kids to help me pay. They were the family that we had in St. Louis, and how I eventually ended up there. When Irene mailed the money for the deposit, he intercepted the package and took possession of the money.

When I asked him about it, he made so many excuses about why he was keeping the money. To me, it seemed like he was trying to keep me from going to school. He had done nothing but ridicule my pursuits. In later years, my father said that it was a mistake he made because he didn't know how to deal with me moving away. His plan backfired to epic proportions. Not only did I leave town, I moved further away than I would've been in Baltimore, and severed all ties with him for years.

That is an example of how the laws of attraction work, even when you are unaware of them. The law of attraction states, "what you focus on the most, you attract." My father's focus was on me moving away, and even though he may have avoided me moving away to Baltimore, he still attracted me moving away, just to a different place.

After fighting with him about my housing deposit, I went to stay with my best friend, Brittany, for a couple of days. Brittany and I had been friends since middle school and best friends since junior year. When I tried to go back home, I was informed that I was no longer welcome. Not only could I not go back, I couldn't step foot inside the house, even to get clothes. My father told me that my grandmother had the final say and she didn't want me in her house. It was his way of deflecting, but it didn't matter.

I doubted if it were even true, but that didn't matter either. All that mattered was that my father had no problem with sending me into the streets, with nothing, not even clothing. A few weeks passed and Irene sent for me, and that's how I ended up in St. Louis. When I left town for good, I had to have a police escort to the house, just to retrieve some clothes.

My father drew a line at that moment, and for years he remained on one side, and I on the other. As far as I was concerned, my father and grandmother were dead in my eyes. I was also determined more than ever to accomplish the goal that I had set, which was graduating from college.

After living in St. Louis for a few months and completing a semester at a college in the city, I knew that I needed to get out on my own, once and for all. Irene was living with her oldest daughter, Kyle, so that's where I ended up also. That was another ghost that haunted me. As a kid, I was always at somebody's house, other than my own, or with someone's parents, other than my own. Kyle had no problems reminding me that I was another mouth to feed. Tired of feeling like a burden, I reached out to my mother and a move to Richmond, VA soon followed. That living arrangement went south even faster than the one in St. Louis.

After a month in Virginia and less than 9 months after I left New Jersey, I was back in St. Louis. This time, I was determined to make my own home, where no one could put me out or make me feel like a burden. There were many times that I struggled trying to live on my own, but I learned how to survive on my own without help from anyone. As years passed, and I maintained, I prided myself on being a survivor, one who could make it through anything. Unaware of the laws of attraction, by labeling myself as a survivor, I was unintentionally inviting more struggle and strife into my life. In order to be this survivor that I prided myself upon being, I would need to survive things. In order to survive things, I would need to go through things. I went from one struggle to the next, always coming out on top and deeming myself stronger than before.

A narrative developed within me that I was alone and on my own. Time and time again, I told myself that I was on my own and no one was there, but me, to help me through my struggles. All I was accomplishing was attracting more loneliness and more struggle into my life. My life was being lived in default mode. Whatever came my way, I accepted, and vowed to overcome. I also developed a deep resentment for my family, especially my mother and father. There were already seeds of resentment planted in me from my childhood and my struggles in young adulthood nurtured further resentment. My father was at the top of my list of people who I resented because I blamed him directly for me ending up in St. Louis in the first place.

After years of struggle, I made a way for myself in St. Louis. When I rose out of the fire, I had love, prosperity, and financial security in my life. I became a student of the new thought movement after stumbling upon *The Secret* movie on Netflix. After watching the film, I began seeking out more and more literature about the law of attraction. Within a matter of months, I had attracted everything into my life that I needed to attract more of the things that I wanted.

I was fully subscribed to the concept that the universe conspires for the benefit of me and the proof was in the way that I was reached. The love that I had for music led me to the song "Happy" by Pharrell Williams, which led me to watch an interview of his with Oprah, in which he lamented on the lessons he learned from reading *The Alchemist*. I downloaded the book on my tablet and read the entire book the very same night. *The Alchemist*, itself, seemed like a cue to me from the universe. The boy in the story had set out on a journey to find a treasure which led him to experiences that he had never anticipated. Convinced that the law of attraction worked and already inclined to search for symbols and hidden meanings, I began looking for cues from the universe and delved deep into controlling my thoughts and attracting all that I wanted in life.

I created a vision board of what I wanted in my future, while focusing on all that I already had. It's very important to practice gratitude for what has been provided, while also looking to the future for what you want to have. The exercise was one of the first things I learned when I began studying the law of attraction. My board contained pictures of weddings, beaches, and money. Those were the things that I wanted to attract and I can attest that they have all manifested. A little more than two years later, I am married, seen the beaches of California and Cancun, and while working a part-time job, unaffiliated with my prior career, I have been more financially stable than ever in my life. More than that would also come into fruition, much of it I hadn't asked for or expected. I expected an amazing journey, but I had no idea that the universe was going to take me where I needed to go via such a scenic route.

When I started learning about the laws of attraction and that right thinking could bring me whatever I wanted, I was a bit afraid that I was engaging in activity that undermined my faith in GOD. It took quite some time for me to reconcile with my faith and my belief in the laws of attraction. Eventually, I discovered how much the words of the bible actually aligned with what I had learned. Finally, I was satisfied when I understood that no matter how much I used the laws of attraction, as powerful as they are, GOD is still the highest power there is. It was okay for me to better myself and my understanding of the universe, because it would never take the place that GOD has in my life. I had two ultra-powerful weapons on my side.

The more and more that it appeared it was working, I struggled to make sense of the experience. Was I really creating this life that I wanted, or was I just getting lucky? Even worse, I thought that I would somehow end up a victim once again. All of these wonderful things were only going to make the blow stronger when my life came crashing back down. There had long been a battle going on in my mind that I attributed to a young life full of traumatic experiences. These mental and emotional demons presented themselves over and over again through the years. Even as I had reached my most prosperous point in my life in my final years in St. Louis, I was still plagued by fear and insecurity which prevented me from being able to fully pursue my dreams or truly believe that I could achieve them. I was still haunted by my childhood.

The more positive my thinking became, the more positive I became. I wanted to rid my life of any negative emotions or feelings. I reconciled with many of my family members and I worked to stop resenting my father. I believed that everything had happened for a reason and that reason would somehow benefit me. My father had gotten close to GOD as he battled cancer and was profoundly different than the man I grew up with. While he was strong in his faith, I noticed that he was also living in default mode when it came to his thoughts. He put all of his recovery in GOD's hands, which could be viewed as true and absolute faith, and resigned to whatever outcome GOD had for him.

That was a huge step for him in comparison to what I had remembered of him growing up. He was ultra-negative about nearly everything when I was a kid. I believe that I inherited that negativity from him and before I learned how it affected my outcomes, I engaged in negative thinking on a regular basis. I even contemplated how his thinking may have affected my sexuality. He avoided hugging me, kissing me, or showing any form of parental affection because he felt it would make me gay. He was so constantly focused on not having a son who was a sissy, among other choice words, but that's exactly what happened. Perhaps, my father's thoughts were transferred to me through the law of attraction. I became what he did not want because he focused on what he did not want as opposed to what he wanted. What he did not want was a son who was homosexual. Through his own thoughts and his speaking, that is what I became. Is it possible that I inherited his negative thoughts and they manifested in my life, even as a child?

I visited my father for his birthday in August 2015, which would be his last. His battle with cancer made me feel sympathy for him for the first time in my life. He was open and vulnerable for the first time in his life and I was open and vulnerable with him in return, for the first time in my life. We had become a father and son for the first time in both of our lives. I got to see the connection that we had as he fought his illness. His body was weakened but his mind remained strong. His strength came from his faith, whereas my strength came from a combination of both spiritual faith and knowledge of the laws of the universe. The glory always went to GOD. This made me wonder how should one balance the understanding of the laws of the universe with an understanding of their faith and if I was doing it correctly. I also wondered about the millions of others out there who are also living in a survival mode, who have no idea or desire to open up to a concept such as law of attraction or even attempt to deal with the negative momentum that tough life experiences can create.

CHAPTER TWO: LAW OF ATTRACTION

When I started studying the laws of attraction and the laws of the universe, I realized I had been using it already without even knowing it. That was powerful to me for two reasons. First, it affirmed that the law of attraction was in fact a legitimate phenomenon. Secondly, I realized where GOD came into place in all of it. We all have the power to attract experiences through the laws of the attraction, yet many of us do not even know or embrace our power. In the absence of this knowledge, GOD, or whomever you believe in, protects you, and guides us all. HE guides those who know and those who do not know their power. For those whose thinking attracts negative things into their lives, HE provides grace and mercy and for those who attract the positive, HE provides favor and abundance.

How I met Travis is a textbook example of how the laws of attraction work. The first step I took was to focus on having love and take my focus off of the lack of love. If you focus on lack, you attract more of the lack. If you focus on what you want, you attract more of what you want. There was already an abundance of love in my life, so I made sure to be grateful of that. I focused on the love that I received from my friends and the love that I received from children whom I worked with. I was always surrounded by loving children, which is what had drawn me to teaching. Even those children who are the most misguided are still full of love. In my first years teaching, I realized that if I focused on the love within the kids, they exuded it more. If I focused on their bad behavior, they behaved badly more frequently. I was using the laws of attraction then and wasn't aware of it.

Next, I stopped listening to K. Michelle or Keyshia Cole songs about how bad love is and engaging in man-bashing conversations with my friends. I didn't stop talking to my friends, I simply redirected our conversations toward what we wanted from love and what it would be like to be in love, and away from the negative.

For all of my young adulthood, I struggled with dating, just as I had struggled with living on my own. Sometimes, I was desperate, and other times I was just stupid. Time after time, I found myself in unproductive and sometimes disastrous situations, none of them leading to anything worthwhile romantically. Most of my twenties, I was single and looking. My friends and I compared our notes on how much dating sucked and how hard it was to find someone good. We all remained single, jumping from situation to situation, sharing story after story. Writing a book full of those stories is one idea I had for my book series. There are so many stories to tell, that I could write my own *Sex and the City*-esque book series. Stay tuned for that.

After so many failed attempts at love, I stopped trying. For just over 5 years, I didn't even date or try to put myself out there. I had all but accepted that love would be an elusive experience in my life. It was to the point that I thought I was just going to end up alone. Maybe some people just weren't meant to have love, and I was one of them. That was going to be the continuation of my sad and pathetic story. A boy who grew up feeling unloved, struggled to find love in adulthood, and just couldn't figure it out. The truth is all the love that I ever needed, I already had. I just needed to learn to love myself.

They say as soon as you stop looking for love, love will find you. What happens is that when you stop looking for love, you realize that you should have never been looking for love in the first place. The very love that you are looking for is love that doesn't require any finding. You already have the love that you are looking for, you just need to direct it inward. You should be loving yourself. Instead of looking for someone to love you, you should look for someone to love. When you find a partner who also loves their own self, they will be looking to love you and not looking for you to love them. Yet, you will love them because that's what you have been looking for---someone to love. You both end up loving each other. It is a perfect design and it all works out wonderfully.

The universe conspired to bring Travis and I together in a way that felt supernatural. What seemed like a setback was a setup for a great blessing! One day, I received a traffic ticket for running a stop sign, in a part of town where you could usually get away with breaking any law. When I appeared at traffic court, I saw a beautiful man who physically embodied everything that I had ever imagined in the man of my dreams. He was the most handsome man I had ever laid eyes on. Travis could have very well jumped directly off my vision board. I assumed he had to be married or at least taken. A man like that had to be spoken for. It never even crossed my mind that he could've be single. Honestly, I didn't even think he was gay.

For a minute, I looked and daydreamed. Then, I went on about my business. His likeness became the prototype for the man that I would want to be with but I never expected to see him again. In just a few minutes, I studied most of his attributes and had a pretty good image of him burned into my memory. Whenever I thought about being in love, I would visualize us together. Not specifically him, but a man who looked just like him, a gay version of him.

Visualization is one of the most powerful tools that you can use to attract anything into your life. Whatever you can see in your mind, can become in life. I told my friends about him and described him from head to toe, further reinforcing my visualization of him and the man that I would attract. I went on with my life as usual and entrusted the universe to do the rest. That was how the process was written about in all the books I had studied about the law of attraction.

A few weeks later, no more than a month, my good friend Mimi and I went out for drinks on a Friday night. Single and always ready to mingle, Mimi and I kept standing Friday and Saturday night plans. Our favorite spot was The Grove, a recently renewed neighborhood that had blended longstanding gay bars with new and trendy mainstream bars. There were also restaurants, shops, and businesses that helped The Grove attract a young and diverse crowd. It was the best of both worlds for us. I could eat crab cakes at my favorite restaurant and then step in and out of whichever crowded bar caught my attention that night. Most of the time, Mimi and I went to the gay bars but we would stumble into the other bars every now and then, usually on our way to another gay bar.

Mimi and I hit up a few new spots before stumbling into one of our frequent stops. By the time we made it to our regular spot, we were already tipsy. The night was very young and it was feeling like one of those nights that wouldn't end until the sun came out. As soon as I stepped foot in the bar, Travis stole my attention from the lights, music, and everyone in my sight line. Of all the years that I had went to bars or clubs, I had never seen Travis before, and now here he was, just weeks after I designated him as the prototype of the man of my dreams. I could not believe my eyes. It *was* the man of my dreams, not a man who looked like the prototype, but it was the actual prototype. He was sitting alone, just waiting for me to come and find him.

Mimi knew him from high school, which made it easy to break the ice. The two of them started chit-chatting about their high school days. He hardly made any eye contact with me and barely engaged me in the conversation. I felt that there was no interest in me. He didn't seem mean, just uninterested. The thoughts in my head began to shift away from excitement toward rejection. That's when I determined myself to hold onto my new teachings. Remain positive and focus on what you want, not what is, I told myself. That is one of the most important tenets of understanding how the laws of attraction work. We shall not put our energy into the things we don't want, or we most surely will manifest more of what we don't want.

Confident that my positive thinking would create results, I decided to nudge him closer to me. I extended Travis an invitation to our next stop and left. He would show up, if it was meant to be. There was no implication that we would ever see each other again, but I trusted the universe. As Mimi and I walked down the street, I kept replaying positive visuals in my head. If the universe wanted us to be together, this wouldn't be our last encounter. I could walk away, move away, or leave the planet and the universe would bring us back together, quickly and easily.

It turned out to be much easier than that. Travis showed up at the next bar and we partied the night away. All the while, I talked to myself and told myself that the universe was working its magic. He didn't know that I had been working diligently to attract him into my life. Nor did he know that I imagined my love story would be a fairy tale. In my mind, I would meet a prince who would kiss me and take all of my pain away. I truly believed that true love's first kiss could erase all of the pain that I had ever experienced.

The entire night, I paid close attention to any cues from the universe and made sure to follow them. We talked about love and our past loves, as well as what we wanted for our futures. In the midst of our conversation, "I believe in fairy tales," came out of his mouth. I was so shocked that

I made him repeat himself. He repeated it and confirmed what I had thought he said. This was all just too easy. I started to feel like I was cheating at some sort of game, or practicing witchcraft. Was this man going to fall in love with me because the universe was forcing him to?

Whenever things seemed to go too well for me, I always allowed thoughts of unworthiness to creep up on me. These thoughts come from past emotions, that even if purged, still leave some residue of negativity. When those thoughts creep up, it's crucial to hold steadfast to your beliefs and tell yourself that you deserve to be happy and that GOD wants you to live a happy and abundant life.

At the end of the night, we exchanged numbers and started texting each other the very next day. He texted me first, which made it easier for me to feel comfortable texting him whenever I wanted to. When you date, there is always this apprehension to be the first person to text or call the other person. I was guilty of being afraid to text or call first. I had my baggage, I'll admit it. I wasn't ashamed of my baggage, I just wanted to fall in love with someone who would help me unpack my bags.

After we started dating, I came clean to my future husband that I had attracted him through the laws of attraction. He was not only pleased but honored that I had gone through so much to bring us together. It was the perfect response. There was something about him that seemed perfect for me from the moment I met him. He wasn't perfect, but he was perfect for me. I knew that he was going to be the man that I always wanted and more. He was not only the man that I had attracted from the universe, but he was the man who I had prayed for. Although the law of attraction may have brought us together, it would take GOD to keep us together. Not even the law of the attraction could have made him stay with me once he met my family and witnessed the layers of dysfunction that were soon to be revealed.

Our courtship was very simple and somewhat traditional. We went to dinners and met for drinks a few times. Of course, things didn't just coast along. By no means, was our courtship perfect, and I questioned if I was making a fool of myself on many occasions. There were moments early on when we were dating that I thought I was going a bit too far with the whole concept of the laws of attraction. It wasn't easy fully accepting that I wouldn't be disappointed once again. It was also difficult to explain to those around me what was motivating me, and why I was approaching this relationship so differently. No one could really understand what I was talking about when I talked about signs, cues from the universe, and positive thoughts. Most of my friends thought I was just so eager for love, that I was convincing myself that he was the one. I didn't blame them, but I also wanted to show them that I knew what I was doing

Travis cancelled a couple of dates and I almost slipped back into my old ways. He was supposed to go with me to a rugby game but backed out after saying that he was too tired. Another night, he said he was too tired for us to have dinner. At one point, our communication even came to a complete standstill without warning. Each instance, I felt my familiar feelings of fear and frustration creep back up on me. I feared that he would turn out like the others had. I was frustrated because I was tired of failures in the romance department. Through it all, an inner voice kept telling me that he was the one and to hold on.

My usual mode of operation would have been for me to sulk in a woe is me state of being. I would have written him off as just like everyone else that had come before him. So many guys had wasted my time that I told myself they all would waste my time. That thinking didn't serve me any good, just as my narrative about being strong didn't serve me any good. Telling myself that I was dealing with the same kind of guy over and over again, only attracted more of the same type of guys, the ones I didn't want, into my life. Things were different this time, I remained patient and held onto my belief that it was all going to work out. How it would work out, I didn't know but I held steadfast to what I believed.

One of the contributors to *The Secret*, talked about sticking to what you know without wavering. She referred to it as "unwavering faith." Love was such a major want of mine, that I was going to do anything to have it. For the first time ever, I was unwavering in my belief that we were going to be together. All of my prior attempts at love were failures that I had anticipated to fail, sometimes as early as the moment that I exchanged names with the other individual.

The first time I ever laid eyes on him was August. We were formally introduced in September. By Halloween, things had slowed down and we were barely communicating. By mid-November, we had been out of touch for a few weeks, which normally would've signaled the end for me. That feeling that he was still the one remained, but I had also come to terms with the idea that he wasn't, or wasn't the one right now. If it was meant to be, it was going to be. If not, I trusted that the universe was going to lead me in the right direction. If I had been wrong and Travis wasn't the one, I still knew that I was getting close to finding the one and I was grateful for that. Regardless of what happened, Travis was still going to be the prototype, and I hadn't abandoned that idea.

We hadn't talked in weeks and then early one chilly, November, Saturday morning, he asked me if I wanted to meet him for coffee. I accepted, but not with the right intentions. My plan was to look amazing, wow him, and then remind him of how much of a fool he was for not wanting to spend every waking moment of his life with me. Things didn't work out that way.

After coffee, we went for lunch, and then to a nearby shop, where we put together our own fragrance oils.

The whole day revealed to me that Travis was much more refined than I had expected. I also realized that we had more in common than I originally thought. After we designed our own oils, I went home, only to end up at his apartment not even an hour later. We spent the rest of that Saturday watching movies and trying to keep our distance on his couch. No, I didn't have sex with him, but I wanted to.

For the five years that I had given up on dating, I had also vowed to remain abstinent until I knew that I was with someone who would be around for the long haul. Sex hadn't gotten me any closer to a commitment in the past, so I decided to approach things differently. I can't say whether or not I would have been able to hold out for five more years, but I had made it that far. My goal wasn't to be a born again virgin, but to wait for the person who I would spend the rest of my life with. Travis was all the man that I had envisioned and it was not easy to contain myself, but I did.

After that day in November, our relationship suddenly took off, and we starting seeing each other on a very regular basis. We both began to open up more, and his behavior started making sense. Travis had just gotten out of a really messed up relationship, which is why he was afraid to get close at the beginning. It explained his cancellations and the unexplained distancing in communication. I did all that I could do to show him that I was different, but I didn't have to. His ex didn't see the value in him, just as my exes hadn't seen the value in me.

We saw an immense value in one another, in the simple things that we did, and the way that we approached love. He had been in a series of relationships before and had even been engaged, to a woman. I use the term *exes* loosely because I had never actually been in a serious relationship before. Yet, our approaches to love were nearly identical. We even had many of the same issues and hang-ups. I feared that would be unhealthy, but it actually made us closer and better able to understand one another's feelings.

Our dates turned into a competition of who could show each other a better time. We must have gone to every awesome restaurant that St. Louis had to offer. I had always thought of myself as an amateur foodie, but Travis showed me some places that I had no idea existed. It was obvious that he had a liking for the finer things in life, and that both surprised and excited me. He was down-to-earth and cultured at the same time. Travis actually took out time and put thought into planning dates and romance. Eventually, we even went to the restaurant that he had backed out of going to months before. He made the date up to me. He was different than any other guy I had ever dated. This man was awesome to me, all rolled up into a handsome package.

By the time Christmas came around, we had reached the point in our relationship where it felt serious, but nothing was official yet. As a single man, I spent Christmas hanging out on my cousin Camille's couch in New Jersey. It seemed right to be around family for the holidays since I was single without any kids. My teaching job afforded me two weeks of freedom between Christmas and New Year's, so I used the time to get away from St. Louis and forget about being an adult. After getting close to Travis, I wanted to take a chance and spend my holiday with him. Even though we had only been seriously dating for a month, something about it felt like the right thing to do.

For the first time in years, I didn't make a trek back to Jersey for the holidays. The last time that I spent Christmas in St. Louis was when I wasn't speaking with anyone in my family at the time. For the first five years that I lived in St. Louis, I didn't keep in contact with anyone, except for when my grandmother died in 2003. We didn't open up the lines of communication again until

Camille graduated from college in 2006. Camille is also my god-sister, and her mother Angela is my god-mother, as well as my aunt. When Camille graduated, Angela reached out and expressed that the moment was bigger than any issues we all were holding onto. I forgave, forgot, and went to see Camille graduate from college. Afterward, we all kept in touch and remained on good terms.

When I graduated from college in 2007, Angela, Camille, and Carl, Angela's husband, along with Shay, Angela's other daughter came to my graduation in St. Louis. After that, the fences seemed to be mended and I started visiting Angela's family during the holidays and summers. Growing up, I always spent a lot of time with my god-parents and god-sisters, so it was easy to transition back into their family unit. They say absence makes the heart grow fonder, and while I hadn't grown fonder of them, we actually got along better after the years of distance.

The issue that had pushed me completely away was actually between my father and I, so I didn't really have a definitive reason to continue to keep my distance from everyone else in his family. I had resentments toward nearly everyone, but I chose to forgive and move on from them. Growing up, I had always felt like everyone was united against me. There never seemed to be anyone on my side when issues arose, and when I was mistreated everyone turned and looked the other way. I never truly felt loved. I was told I was loved, but I could never accept it for some reason. My heart never believed what it was being told.

As strongly as I felt, I dismissed those feelings and decided it was easier and better for everyone for me to forgive. I wasn't ready just yet to forgive my mother, father, and sister, but I had to start somewhere. It was a good decision to try and release my feelings but I neglected to actually dispose of them correctly. I pushed them to the back of my mind and dismissed a lot of what I felt as growing pains or feelings that everyone has. At that time, I was coming into my own as a professional and it was the first time in my life that I was truly happy with who I was as a person. Because of timing, I swept all of the negative in my life under a rug and chose to move forward. It was a time when I wanted to choose happiness and gratitude. I was grateful to have god-parents and god-sisters, so why hold on to issues?

Deciding not to go to Jersey that Christmas wasn't a hard decision to make, which says a lot about the actual state of my relationship with my family at the time. In an instant, I chose to spend the holidays with a relative stranger rather than them.

It felt good to me to feel like I had exercised forgiveness. The only problem was that I didn't really hold anyone in my family accountable for my feelings. My mother, father, and even my sister were the only family I was holding accountable. Everyone else, I basically let off the hook. Nothing had truly been resolved. All I had done was diverted all of my resentment to my mother and father. On the surface, everyone was getting along, but there were plenty of underlying issues.

Travis and I made plans for the rest of my holiday time to visit Memphis, Tennessee for New Year's Eve. It was going to be our first trip together, and my first trip ever with a love interest. Christmas Eve was also the first night that we slept in the same bed together. We still hadn't had any sexual interaction, but it definitely felt like a major step in our relationship. On Christmas Day, we exchanged gifts, even after we agreed that we wouldn't. I gave him a scarf and some socks which I thought would be appropriate for someone who I wasn't supposed to buy a gift for. Travis' gift was much more thoughtful than I was prepared for. He gave me a bracelet in the shape of cross that had my name engraved on it. He knew about how hard I was working on building my faith, and he was listening.

A couple days after Christmas, we went to Memphis for five days. It was the first time that we were going to spend that much time with each other alone. It was also the first time that he would see me completely exposed. I can't remember how I ended up yelling but there was drinking involved. A lot. Some very small disagreement led me to expose all the insecurities that I didn't even know were there myself.

Travis and I were on the verge of something amazing and the issues that I had thought were gone resurfaced. I didn't know how to deal with something such as wonderful as love happening to me. Feelings of unworthiness and fear crept up in me and took me over. Somehow, I ended up screaming and yelling, and did everything I could to push him away. It was self-sabotage in the worst way. He was too good to be true and too good for me. I told him to leave me, that he might as well. He would leave me eventually, and I was just setting myself up for failure, by continuing to get close to him.

My yelling eventually turned into uncontrollable crying. I was sure that he was going to break up with me and leave me. But he didn't. He grabbed me and held me. He pressed my cheek to his chest and I cried until I could cry no more. He didn't leave me. He didn't yell at me. He rubbed my back. He comforted me. He kissed me. He loved me.

The rest is history. The next morning, he farted for the first time in front of me. He looked embarrassed at first until I burst into laughter. He said he had been holding it in for days. It was symbolic. We both were holding in something and we both had let it out.

We hit the city and the casinos in nearby Tunica, Mississippi. Everything felt perfect and I was more excited than ever. On our way home, I started to feel sad when I thought about it all coming to an end. I didn't want to leave from him. I told Travis that I didn't want to leave his side and he lit up. He told me the same thing in return. So, we stopped at my house, picked up my clothes, and I spent the night at his apartment. I started picking my clothes up everyday after work and staying at his house every night. From that day on, we were together every single day. It was the kind of love that I had always wanted. He was like my best friend, or even a brother.

Two months later in February 2015, we moved in together. My lease at my apartment had expired and Travis suggested that we might as well move together, since I was there every night. Everything started falling into place, which let me know that we were truly in perfect alignment. I saw it as a new chapter in my life, purging old belongings, feelings, and even relationships. It was all happening so quickly but it felt right, as it had felt from the very first time that I laid eyes on him.

CHAPTER THREE: FROM SCRATCH

Living together turned out to be easier than I would have imagined. As the months passed, we grew closer and closer. Traveling became our main hobby, with eating out following closely behind. We went to Chicago, Las Vegas, and visited my family in New Jersey. We designated Memphis as the place we fell in love and went back for Valentine's Day as well as the next New Year's Eve. Eventually, we became sexually involved, but only after we were best friends. It felt like we did everything the way we were supposed to. I felt loved without any confusion or any doubt in my mind. When Travis told me he loved me, I understood it, accepted it, and truly believed it.

Falling in love had been the most important goal in my life as I felt it had eluded me since birth. Once I had it, it became my most important duty to sustain it and continue to grow together. As my relationship with Travis grew, I also grew tremendously. In a very short period of time, I outgrew most of what I had surrounded myself with. All other things didn't seem as important nor as fulfilling.

My job began to feel like nothing more than a daily dose of stress. Many of the people who I considered friends no longer appealed to me. I realized that I had surrounded myself with many people just to avoid boredom in my single life. Some of my friends didn't seem to be open to the more evolved, in-love, version of me. Now that I was happy, I wanted to only include people and experiences that furthered my happiness. I found myself purging energy, things, and people who no longer seemed to fit into my my new life. Anyone or anything that wasn't working toward my happiness started fading from my life.

Some things went easier than others. My job was

harder to purge than anything else. Each day, I pushed back diligently against the negative environment that I was working in and the negative thoughts that filled my head, whenever I was there. However, I was unable to completely snap my negative thinking, even though I had become aware of how powerful my thoughts were. I came to the conclusion that I simply didn't want to be there and forcing myself to be somewhere that I didn't want to be was counterproductive. I just wanted to go.

When I became a teacher, it was a decision made during survival mode. It was a comfortable career that would allow me to live a stable and responsible life. Teachers were respected and I could do something positive in the lives of many. I've always loved children and I grew into being a master teacher on accident. As long as I was doing something to empower the children I worked with, I was successful. It was the universe that led me into teaching because I needed to learn more about life than I had up until that point. It was GOD that wanted me to teach to help reach those who are so often unreachable. It felt like I was doing what GOD wanted me to do and when it no longer felt that way, I knew that I had to get out. I didn't desire to survive anymore, I wanted to thrive.

In October of 2015, my stress and frustration physically manifested into illness. I broke out in a painful and disgusting rash which I later found out was shingles. The emergency room doctor could only stare in disbelief that I had developed this condition at age 32. He delivered the life-changing news that I could only be in this condition as a result of extreme stress. My primary doctor went further and placed me on high-blood pressure medicine, asserting that I had heart attack levels of blood pressure on multiple visits. I was killing myself, either because of the stress of my job or the self-inflicted perception of stress that I had developed. After ten years and three advanced degrees in my field, I came to the conclusion that my career was no longer working out for me. I was being nudged to move in a different direction, the direction that my heart wanted to go in.

Love has the power to reawaken the things that a lack of love can silence or deaden. In my case, having someone fall in love with all of me built confidence in the talents and dreams that I had buried deep within me. True intimacy exposes one's true self and my true self is an artist, writer, and creative being. All of the dreams and talents which I had put on the back burner and then buried completely were rebirthed through love. My dreams were the things that Travis loved most about me. The presentation that I gave to the world is what attracted Travis to me, but it was my true self, my true heart, the real me, that he loved.

Travis' seemingly perfect alignment with my dreams and goals only further solidified my belief in the law of attraction and put me in a fervor. We started tossing up a few cities as places to relocate but weren't completely sure which place we wanted to commit to. Before I knew it, we were flying to Phoenix for his job interview. He had gotten a tip about a job, sent in a resume, and was called in to meet with human resources. We immediately fell in love with the geography, the palm trees, and the people. There was something about Phoenix that felt so right, that I knew it had to be another cue from the universe.

I had an interview myself a few weeks later, which gave us another excuse to return to beauty and warm weather. By now, it was December, and Phoenix was a beautiful and sunny escape from the cold weather in St. Louis. It was obvious that I was more than qualified for any job related to education. Not only did I have years of experience, I had just received my Educational Specialist's degree on the 11th of December. As qualified as I was, something told me that I wasn't going to get the job I applied for nor did I really, truly want it.

I didn't get the job. The universe responded accordingly. If I had gotten that job, I would've never been able to keep focused on what I was being called to do, which was writing. GOD has given me gifts and the universe conspires to help me use those gifts. That conspiracy, on behalf of the universe, led to Travis being offered a job, in Phoenix, just weeks later, with a start date in February of 2016.

On Christmas Day 2015, just a year after we spent our first Christmas together, we spent our last Christmas in St. Louis. My gift for Christmas was a teddy bear with a miniature backpack. Inside his backpack was a diamond ring. Travis proposed to me. That was the first time I understood what it felt like to be still. Stillness allows us to see what we have and it opens us up to gratitude. Being still allows GOD to answer our prayers, and the universe to present us with the signs we need. If we are always in motion, moving toward the next thing, we can miss those answers and signs.

Being still had always been difficult for me. It required me to do nothing, which for me was the hardest thing to do. Or should I say not do? The life experiences that I had always required some sort of response, plan, or action. I could create a vision board to help me visualize or make a list of all that I'm grateful for. Those exercises required me to do something, but being still required me to wait and believe. It was an act of surrender that required vulnerability and true faith. It was the one tenet of the new thought movement that I struggled to grasp.

As I looked at my engagement ring and into the eyes of my future husband, I fully understood stillness. Stillness was about that very moment and what it means. That moment meant that Travis wanted to be with me, just the way I was for the rest of our lives. It meant that I would never have to want for love as I had wanted for all of those years, which seemed endless. It meant that anything that happened from that moment on would be secondary to us. Life, death, and everything in between was secondary to our love. I could be still because whatever would happen in the future, I was going to have support and love in my corner.

Later that day, I called Angela to wish her a happy holiday. I also told her about our engagement. She sounded genuinely happy for us and shared the news with Camille, Shay, and Carl. I also spoke to my father that day, but I was too nervous to share the news. As much as we had reconciled, his homophobic language and approach to masculinity remained burned in my memory. The fact that he had immersed himself in church while battling cancer, only made me more uneasy about telling him that I would be marrying a man. I did tell him about our decision to move to Phoenix, which he lauded us for. He was more than excited that I had decided to pursue my writing. Surprisingly, he was also very supportive of the idea that I was going to quit my job. He recommended that I got out as soon as possible and go after all of my dreams.

My plan was to leave my job in January, but as the new year approached, I opted for a fresh start to 2016. There was no way that I was taking that negative energy with me into another year. After I told my father about wanting to quit, he came up with a plan that he described as making the best out of a bad situation. His idea was that I would take a leave from work without having to quit. We could use his illness as an excuse for me to take time off. I had no intention of ever going back, but at least his plan would make leaving less messy for me, than just up and leaving. I figured that I should definitely take heed to advice given by someone who is terminally ill.

During the previous year or so, my father and I had started to open up more with one another. We weren't close but we were on better terms. In the months leading up, I started to recognize how much we had in common with one another. He had a great deal of tenacity when it came to dealing with his circumstances, something that I recognized in myself. We made the most out of any situation, no matter how bad. "If I have cancer, why not take advantage of it?" he suggested. This man was pretty clever about things, a trait that I too possessed.

Just days after the start of the New Year, Travis and I made the trek to New Jersey to put my father's plan into action. His condition appeared to have vastly improved since we saw him for his birthday in August. His spirits were high and there was definitely a vibe that he could beat his illness. If nothing else, he was going to continue to live with it and keep fighting it.

I was in awe at times of how independent he wanted to be as sick as he was. He didn't want me to stay with him during chemotherapy and insisted that he could catch the bus home. He saw no reason for me to drive back to Philadelphia to pick him up from chemotherapy. There was no question that he was resilient, but I wondered if he was being too resilient. Did he need to rest more and allow his body to try and heal?

He was on the move as if he was 20 years younger and saw no reason to make any changes to his daily life. I was shocked that he had conceded to move into an apartment for senior citizens, after vowing to remain in the house he had lived in all his life. It was the same house that I was raised in and that he grew up in as a child. It was also the same house that I was thrown out of at age 17. To me, it was just a structure. I had no emotional attachment to it, other than the painful memories I had from childhood. To him, the house represented his lineage and inheritance as the eldest male with our family name.

My father had lived his whole life anticipating that the house would be his someday. When my grandmother died, it became his by default but legally remained in my grandfather's name, who had long been deceased. The house wasn't structurally sound and lacked modern amenities that people in the 1970's would've expected. I believe that some of the materials in the house and even the air may have been toxic. It was just a theory of mine, but I wondered if the house may have even contributed to his illness. His mother died of cancer, in 2003, after living in that house, and here he was suffering the same fate. Even if my theory was true, it wouldn't have persuaded him to leave the house. He had been in his apartment for a few months, but he still caught a bus to the dilapidated house on a daily basis. His dog still lived there and he would make sure to visit and feed him. Sometimes, he would go to the house just to sit on the front porch, like he always had.

Cancer hadn't changed much about his daily life or his personality either. He remained as rude, arrogant, and visceral as he was all his life. If he had suddenly toned himself down, I would've been worried. Church had softened him up a little but he remained steadfast in his assertion of who he was. Being rude, arrogant, and visceral made him who he was, and he was proud of those attributes. Although he had lived his entire life in his mother's house, you couldn't tell him that he wasn't the man of the house or the big man about town.

When my grandmother died, Angela positioned herself as his closest relative and was there for him on a regular basis. Yet, he still presented himself as a boisterous, take-charge alpha male, who didn't need help from anyone. He and Angela butted heads on a regular basis as they both struggled to find a balance in their relationship. Angela helped my father financially but my father didn't see that as cause for him to be subordinate or subservient to his little sister. As he grew older and sicker, their relationship went from complicated to dysfunctional, and often toxic.

When my father and I were estranged, I wasn't privy to anything that went on between he and Angela. When I started talking to the both of them, I often found myself in the middle of their disagreements. My father would express his frustration with what he felt was a lack of respect for him because he was dependent upon her. Angela would express frustration with what she felt was not only a lack of appreciation but the audacity that he would have to insult her. Angela felt as though because she was always by his side, the least he could do was temper his tongue and scale back insults. My father insisted that Angela put them both in positions to be insulting to one another and that it was unfair for him to be expected to absorb her insults, just because he needed her more than she needed him. He refused to let her talk to him any kind of way because she was helping him out.

When Angela would tell me about one of their fights, I could identify with how she felt a lot of the times. My father's words definitely cut and could cause you to give up on trying to have any kind of relationship with him. That was my own personal experience and also the catalyst for my bias. Angela was no angel, but I gave her the benefit of the doubt because she did do a lot for him. She had done a lot for me as well, so I believed that she had our best interest at heart.

If my father told me about an argument they had, I could understand his point of view, but I never felt as sympathetic to him as I did to Angela. Part of the reason was that he never presented himself as a sympathetic figure. He had made it his duty to present himself as someone who didn't need anyone, didn't care about anyone's feelings, and didn't have to answer to anybody for what he said.

My father had complex relationships with all of his sisters and their relationships with one another were just as complex. They all gossiped about what the others were doing and when one got mad at the other, the other siblings were let in on the details from both sides. My father would confide in his other sisters, Irene and Etta, about his problems with Angela, fully aware that Irene and Etta had their own issues with her. All of them harbored deep seeded resentment toward each other. Some of their issues stemmed from as far back as when they were children. I guess that's what most families do, but it only caused confusion about who really felt what about whom.

Just days before Travis and I arrived in Jersey, Angela called to tell me that she was "done" with my father. She was fed up with him and said that he was too toxic and nasty for her to deal with. Angela decided that she was not going to pay his phone bill or cable bill until he learned how to speak to her respectfully. This conflict was a prime example of how things usually went when the two of them butted heads. In her opinion, he should choose his words differently, or face consequences.

As usual, I couldn't take a side in the matter because I could understand them both completely. Fortunately for me, I had put a lot of effort toward learning to understand multiple perspectives in a disagreement. It was a skill I perfected, refereeing disagreements between fifth graders. But something stuck out in this conversation with Angela. She made a reference to my father acting differently when I came around. She felt as though he became cocky and disregarded others because he knew that I would be there soon. When I was around, he felt as though I could take the place of the people he normally depended on, namely Angela and Irene. I thought it was a very interesting observation and comment for someone to make about how a parent acts when their child comes around. Was he wrong for feeling more empowered when his only child was around?

After driving for 20-something hours, we rolled into New Jersey in the early morning hours. I told my father I would take him to the doctor that morning when I arrived. I spent the entire first day at the cancer center with my father. It was disheartening to watch patient after patient file in for care. Many of them looked like they had all but given up. I wondered what their lives were like before and how they would be after. Who would actually beat cancer and who would lose? And why would the losers lose and the winners win? I knew how the laws of attraction worked but I wondered if any of the patients knew. I just wanted every single person in the waiting room to know what I knew about the laws of attraction and for them to begin thinking their way to health.

My father stood out from the other patients because he appeared to be much cooler and calmer than any of them appeared to be. It was another moment when he reminded me of myself. He actually looked happy and unbothered by his ordeal. He joked around and flirted with every nurse, which was shocking, since he was known for being very hard on the looks of women. I guess when you're faced with your own mortality, a lot of your old ways subside. He had become more likable than I had ever remembered.

I didn't tell my father about the conversation that Angela and I had because I didn't want to be put in the middle. The more that I thought about it, the more uncomfortable I began to feel about some of the things that Angela said. This argument made me feel a bit differently than usual. Maybe I was more sympathetic towards my father because of his condition but I didn't think Angela was right this time. I wouldn't treat a person that I loved that way, especially not one who was terminally ill. As wrong as my father may have been, it seemed to be a bit extreme for someone to subject a terminally ill person to anything that could cause great stress, such as having their phone cut off.

Over the years, my father had built up plenty of resentment toward Angela. Some of his resentment came from the way that he felt my grandmother and Angela treated him. He was always asserting his manhood because he felt that they treated him like a child. He also resented Angela for the role that he felt she played in our relationship. He felt that Angela was part to blame for the wedge that was between he and I because Angela and I had grown closer while he and I remained distant.

As we sat and waited for his doctor, my father brought up the argument between he and Angela, and of course his story was much different than hers. Actually, his story sounded more realistic than hers. In her story, she was tired of being pushed around by her brother whom she did nothing but help. In his story, they had both said some mean things, and he ultimately went too far. His story made more sense to me. That was the family that I knew. Unfortunately for him, he was in need of her, more than she was in need of him.

It must have been the changes that I had recently made in my life that caused me to begin to see things differently. I began questioning motives, of myself and Angela. Why now would my father's sister deem it necessary to teach him a lesson about the way that he talked to people? Everyone let him be the way that he was all of his life. So, why now, when he was ill would anyone expect him to become a person that he never was before? I certainly didn't expect him to be different and he didn't expect me to be different either.

I too was also holding resentment toward Angela which may have blocked my ability to be completely impartial. When I visited Jersey over the summer, Angela said something to me that stuck with me. Somehow, a trivial discussion became an even more trivial argument. The family's favorite trivial argument is always about who is related to who in the small town or what year someone graduated from high school. No one in the family can accept being wrong, so a ridiculous topic such as that can often lead to personal insults. When you add alcohol into the situation, things can quickly go south.

After going back and forth about who was related to who in town, Angela started spewing some really mean things at me. I told her I refused to go low like she was. After she continued to say hurtful things, I fought back by telling her that she couldn't hurt me with her words. That was apparently too much for her to swallow, because she went in for the kill. "I can't hurt you. I was there for you when no one gave a f--- about you." she said. I couldn't believe the conversation went that far in her mind. "Your mom and dad were both f--ked up," she followed up.

Not only did the conversation and the petty disagreement not warrant her statements, it was one of the first times that Travis was around the family. It was embarrassing and uncomfortable for both he and I. The silver lining was that he got to see all of what I had went through as child for himself. You can explain something to someone in words, but when they see it firsthand, they truly understand. When I thought about how she had made me feel, I realized that my father may have been right this time. Angela felt that because she had done things for me and my father that she was able to speak to us in anyway that she wanted, even if that meant degrading us.

If Angela had said that to me years ago, I would've internalized it. I had already changed when she said it and I saw it just for what it was. Her words were not a reflection of me or my parents, she was just mean. Her intent behind what she said was more important than what she said. Why would she want me to think that my mother and father were not there for me? As I recalled my resentment to Angela and our argument, I knew that my father was not the only participant in the hurling of insults, nor was their nasty argument one-sided, as Angela had tried to present it.

When my father and I first discussed my move and taking leave from work, he told me that I should make sure that I keep anything we talked about strictly between us, that included the visit, and the leave that I would be taking.

His exact words were "Please keep it between us." He said that his sisters would find a way to make things negative. I didn't ask him what he meant by that, I just followed his directions as he requested and kept quiet about it all. Soon enough, I would find out exactly how negative they really were and what he really meant.

CHAPTER FOUR: FAMILY MATTERS

The moment I e-mailed my leave paperwork to human resources, I immediately felt free. I had given so much of myself to others during my time as a teacher, that I had forgotten what it was like to put myself first. Having the freedom to do what nurtured me, excited me and reawakened feelings that I had long suppressed. I felt young and determined. I felt that I could do whatever I wanted to as long as I put my mind to it.

To celebrate, we decided to drive up to New York City. Our future was in Arizona, and we knew that it might have been a while before we made it back east. It would only take us a little more than an hour drive from where my father lived. Travis had already accepted a new position in Phoenix, so he was using up his vacation days from his old job. We were both free and able to do whatever it was we wanted to do, at least for the next few weeks. It seemed like it was the perfect time to just be lovers.

The energy in New York is always invigorating and makes you feel that any and everything is possible. While I was already feeling that same energy inside, I wanted to cultivate more of it. Once upon a time, I believed that I would somehow end up as a New Yorker, someday in my life. I think New Yorkers are born to be New Yorkers, even if they aren't born in New York. There's something about the people that end up in New York that connects them all. I always had an image in my head that I would move there and become a successful writer, actor, or some kind of artist.

My first trip to New York was in the 7th grade, on my 7th grade class trip. As close as we were, living in New Jersey, the family never made regular trips, or really talked much about New York. Where I grew up, people acted like going two miles away was a long trip. I didn't have that same small town mindset, but I didn't realize how close New York was either. I went to New York for a second time in 10th grade for a writing competition, and my love for New York was solidified. It wasn't the city itself that I loved; I loved that it was a place where anyone could do or be anything.

Like so many single gay guys and gals in the early 2000s, I was hooked on *Sex and The City*. It was like someone had personified the caricature of myself who lived in my head. It also seemed that someone had perfectly chronicled my struggles of being single. I imagined myself moving to New York to live out my life as a jet-setting writer, just like Carrie Bradshaw. If you had asked me back then, I would've told you that Carrie Bradshaw and I both were going to stay single forever. Fast forward to 2016 and I wasn't single anymore, I was engaged, and love was changing the way I was viewing the world.

Travis and I spent a day in the city, sightseeing, eating, and breathing in the vibrancy. I couldn't deny the vibrations that I felt and I wondered how the universe was able to balance all of the energy of all of these people in such a confined space. There was evidence everywhere that the energy of all the people in New York city had manifested to create a magnificent spectacle. Greatness was everywhere, in the buildings, in the art, and the talent that filled the streets. New York was the greatest city in the world and everyone there was encapsulated in that energy.

As amazing as New York City is, love definitely transformed how I viewed the city. New York was still very much awesome, but it was also over-the-top, overpriced, and overcrowded. I was no longer as excited by the constant stimulation or even the magnificence that was New York City. In fact, I would have rather spent my time cozying up in a secluded cabin. Arizona had presented me with a view of nature and beauty that I hadn't appreciated before experiencing it. Still, the city reminded me of dreams that I once had and continued to reawaken the creative forces that were re-emerging.

As we headed back to Jersey later that evening, I realized how much I had changed and that I was still changing. Just the day before, I was questioning how my father was being treated by Angela. That was a first. Love had definitely made me softer, but what else had love changed about me? While I was amazed at how much I had changed at the same time I was reminded of who I used to be. I felt I was balancing who I was with who I was becoming. There were things about me that I ***shouldn't*** have changed, mainly my desire to be creative. New York seemed like just a fun day trip, but when the universe is working on your behalf, even the most unexpected events can have an effect on you. New York reminded me of the artist I was in 10th grade, who wanted to be a writer, entered writing contests, and won!

Why had I given up on him and all the dreams that he had? Immediately, I began jotting down notes for a project that I had no real direction for. All I knew was that I wanted to harvest the energy that I felt in that moment and turn it into something that would not only express what I was feeling but could inspire others. My concept was titled *From Scratch*. *From Scratch* would chronicle my journey as I became a celebrity chef and food blogger. It was also an attempt to combine two of my passions together and pursue them both simultaneously. Writing had been my talent since I was a kid, and cooking had become a creative outlet for me more recently.

Coming to terms with letting go of all that I had achieved and worked for before was the hardest part of transitioning. In order to reach for and grasp new accomplishments, I had to let go of all of my education and career accomplishments up to that point. The last thing I wanted to accept was that all of my hard work would be in vain. All of my years of school and the resume I had built would feel like it had all been for nothing, if I was truly going to commit to being a writer. *From Scratch* seemed like a catchy concept, but actually following through with it meant it would take on a deeper meaning. It was cute on paper, but from scratch, meant starting over with nothing.

Ever harder would be letting go of all the misconceptions that I had held onto for much of my life. Of course, in order for me to let go of the misconceptions, I would first need to realize them. That process of realization had only just begun for me and I still had a long way to go. GOD was definitely working on me and it was evident through all of the signs being presented by the universe. My biggest responsibility was to work on being still so that I could see how my steps were ordered. GOD would do the rest.

Over the years of being me, I've realized that I respond better to pressure. It hasn't been by choice but more by necessity. I do better when I'm pushed, blocked, or put in a position where I have to act quickly. Sometimes, when I seek rapid growth or progress, I purposely put myself under pressure so that I make sure that I do well. This approach has gotten me through multiple degree programs in college and spurred much of my personal growth. While many frown upon procrastination, I would embrace it at times, knowing that I could do better at something at the last minute. It doesn't work for everyone but it has worked for me.

I decided that I would take that same approach to letting go of my misconceptions. I hoped that by putting myself under the pressure, I would let go of things quicker. Not only would I need to let go of misconceptions, but my thoughts and feelings would also have to change. The most prominent feelings that I needed to change were the ones I had about my own parents.

For all of my adult life, I had told myself a

narrative about my parents. I was going to let that go. I told myself that my father and mother had too many issues to love me the way that I wanted to be loved. I also told myself that my mother was not willing to fight hard enough for me, or she was too lazy to go out of her way to fight for me. Whether this narrative was true or not, continuing to hold onto this thinking would only attract and manifest more negativity. Besides, starting over from scratch meant that I had to wipe the slate clean.

I wanted letting go to be easy but I questioned myself. I always questioned myself. It was just what I had become accustomed to doing. I asked myself, Would I be lying to myself or pretending? Was I letting them off the hook too easy? I came to the conclusion that it really didn't matter. The time had come to let go. Even if I had the right to still be hurt, or the right to air my grievances, I was choosing not to. Instead, I chose to be happy with who I was and who I was going to become. I couldn't erase what had already happened in my life, it was already written. However, I had the power turn the page.

Much of what I felt about my parents had been influenced by other members of the family. It wasn't the only factor in the resentment that I had, but I had heard a lot as a child that I shouldn't have. My mother and father's marriage was often the subject of family fodder and ridicule. My grandmother and Angela used to down my mother just for their own entertainment. My mother was attacked for being gay, being on welfare, or even because of where she grew up. They never attacked her in person but it was always done directly in front of me. They made sure I heard them.

Irene and Etta lived out of state, so I don't remember hearing them say much about my mother, but I remember the things that Angela and my grandmother said about my mother very vividly. Angela lived the closest in proximity to us and to my grandmother, so she was always around or on the phone with my grandmother. They held nothing back without any regard for me or how I felt about the things they said about my mother or father.

Honestly, I didn't care much about what they said about my father because he had emotionally detached himself from me for as long as I could remember. I also resented him because he was the one who I blamed for keeping me away from my mother. When they talked negatively about my mother, it used to create a fire in my stomach. I felt like I hated them. It seemed like they did it more just to hurt me.

They seemed to take pleasure in destroying my mother's image in front of me. I theorized why they would talk so abusively about a child's mother right in front of the child. Did they want me to distance myself from her and align directly with them? Perhaps they thought that a child would lose their love for their mother if she were not around and others were acting in her place. Could it be possible that these people were so self-absorbed that they wanted me to disown my own mother for their own self-satisfaction? Maybe they had purely sociopathic motives. Maybe they wanted to watch me, a child, squirm, as they degraded the closest person to me. Whatever their motive was, I could not defend myself or my own mother.

After years, I became immune to it and eventually, even stopped caring what they said about her or anyone else, for that matter. I'll never know what motivated them but I will never forget what happened. I will never forget how they associated anything negative about me to my mother. If my room was dirty, they would say I was trifling like her. If I told a lie, they said I was a liar like her. If I was sneaky, I was sneaky like her. If I dropped something, I was clumsy like her. Anything that they deemed an inconvenience, I must have inherited from my mother's side of the family.

I was very clumsy as a boy. I felt like a

bumbling idiot as a child and was pretty much a nervous wreck because of them. Every single interaction I had with my family as a child unnerved me because somehow I knew that I would be ridiculed and attacked by them. My father never came to my rescue either and when he felt bullied by them he would turn around and take it out on me. I suppose he didn't want to stand against their united front. The way that they talked to him and diminished him, in combination with his lack of affection and emotional detachment, caused me to view him more like a big brother, rather than a father. There were times when I would get in trouble for things that he did around the house. He knew that it was his fault but he was so afraid of getting a tongue-lashing from his mother, that he would sit by and watch me get punished for something he did. He was childish to me, and I didn't have much respect for him during my childhood.

So, I grew into an awkward child with fear and shame embedded into my every waking moment. I was afraid of being myself and never received praise for anything. I started lying about every mistake I made because I knew that I would be ripped to pieces for any mistake that I made. That didn't help me. I earned the reputation of being a liar and constantly was accused of doing everything imaginable. Even if I hadn't done anything, it didn't matter. Once you're labeled as a liar, no one will believe anything that you say.

As I grew older, I was labeled with more negative traits, labels that I did not earn nor deserve. Not only was I liar, but I was labeled as sneaky, manipulative, and opportunistic. My father never came to my defense and saw their attacks on me as opportunities for him to get on their good side. He would either join them against me or get them to join him against me. While my father was physically there in the home, emotionally he was absent, and I was left to fend for myself against everyone. I'm blessed that I was able to overcome the emotional abuse, but I developed a large amount of resentment toward my father for his part in the abuse and toward my mother for not being there to protect me.

My mother and I hadn't put any effort into our relationship since I was a child. With my father, I felt that it was only right that we did some kind of work based upon the history that we had with one another. Because he was always present in even the minimalist form, we had some sort of foundation to work from. My mother and I, on the other hand, had no foundation of any kind. She hadn't even felt compelled to tend to any duties as a mother. She was absent financially, emotionally, and physically. She was never in attendance when I needed her nor did she seem to make an effort. Needless to say, I was having a harder time letting go of the resentment I had towards my mother, than I did with my father.

Instead of beating myself up, I accepted that it would be more challenging and take longer with my mother. It took 32 years to learn the importance of living in the moment. As long as I tried in the moment and tried again in the next moment, that momentum would build and eventually things would turn.

With this in mind, I made arrangements for my sister to bring my mother to New Jersey, to meet with my father. My mother moved to Virginia when I was very young and never moved back to New Jersey. The goal for having her come to New Jersey was twofold. I wanted my father to have an opportunity to make amends with her, as I thought it would help with his healing. It would also give me an opportunity to take the first steps toward building the momentum that I needed to rebuild some sort of relationship with my mother.

My mother agreed to meet with my father at a local pizza place, just a few steps away from his apartment. As we waited in the parking lot for my sister to arrive, I realized that this meeting would mark the first time I saw my mother in almost 15 years. It would also be the first time that I witnessed my mother and father sit and have a meal together. Anxiety built as the magnitude of this meeting sunk in. In my own way, I was replacing negative memories, thoughts, and narratives with positive ones.

It didn't matter how many bad thoughts I had about my parents or the feelings that they had toward each other. At that moment, which was the present at the time, there was going to be a positive interaction, a positive memory, and positive feelings would arise from it. Never had I imagined that I would be having a family dinner, for the first time at age 32, with my mother, father, and sister, but it was happening. From this, I realized that it's never too late for anything, and that anything is truly possible in life.

Almost 33 years ago, my parents met at a bar in Camden, New Jersey. The city has been a perpetual ghetto for decades where crime, drug use and trafficking, poor education and lack of health care oppress the largely African-American and Latino population of the city. At the time when my parents met, he had many advantages over many men in Camden. He lived in a different town, which had a much better reputation. He worked a good job, something that was harder to come by during the Reagan years, and still is in present-day Camden. He had a fair complexion, which was heavily overhyped in the 1980's. My mother who came from an impoverished family in Camden saw him as a way to a better life.

They began dating and were probably a better match than either of them realized. Not because they were in love but because they were both looking for something that the other could've provided. My mother was struggling with being gay and wanted a husband who could provide her with a normal life and stability.

She was raised in Camden by her grandparents

after losing both of her parents as a newborn. My maternal grandmother committed suicide after my mother's father, who was actually married to another woman other than my grandmother, died in an accident. My mother says she grew up in poverty and incest and was raped by her grandfather on many occasions. My mother left home at age 17, just like myself, and says that she was raped again by another man. This man was my sister's father. After being a victim of rape again, she says she became a lesbian.

When my father met her, he too needed someone to love him unconditionally. He looked good on paper but he came with his own set of issues as well. His family was highly critical of the choices he made and often bullied him. He was looked down upon after he made a near fatal mistake during his senior year of high school. His mother never truly let him forget about his mistake and his family sent him mixed messages of support and disdain for what he had done.

When he was 17, he was involved in an accident while being chased by police. He worked in an auto body shop and would take the cars that were in the shop for joy rides. Everyone knew what he was doing but no one advised him to stop. One day, he took a car and he was reported to the police. The ensuing chase caused him to flip over the median in the road and he was severely injured, nearly dying.

My father spent a year in the hospital undergoing an intensive rehabilitation. He was given a metal plate in his head which would cause him to have seizures until the day he died. He also had to become left-handed and one-handed as he would never be able to open his right hand out of a fist. The injury to his leg caused him to walk with a pronounced limp for the rest of his life.

Before his accident, Irene described him as the "golden boy" of the family. That all changed after his accident. No one in the family came to visit him for most of the time that he was hospitalized because he had shamed the family in the town. Irene described the change in the family attitudes toward him as a "fall from grace." Since no one came to see him, Irene made sure to visit him every day and eventually took up nursing after spending so much time at the hospital.

When I first moved to St. Louis, Irene used to tell me stories all about what it was like for him in the hospital. It was her way of trying to bridge the gap between my father and I after he put me out on the street. If I could understand what he had been through, I would be able to understand why he treated me the way he had. If I knew of his plight, I would know that he loved me but struggled with his own demons. What I realize now, is that both of my parents suffered traumatic experiences at age 17, which altered their relationship with their families forever. My ejection from the home at 17 continued that rite of passage.

My mother and father would marry each other and bring me into this world under much duress. My sister was 5 years old when I was born. She was happy to have a baby brother and my father as her stepfather. My sister's father was not around and our mother told her that she was conceived out of rape. She called my father "daddy," a term of endearment that I have never used. He was actually nicer to my sister, than he was to me, because she was a girl. Everyone told me that he hadn't gotten along with his own father, so he treated me the only way that he knew how, based on what he had experienced.

My sister grew up with this notion that I was afforded so much opportunity as opposed to the lifestyle that my mother provided her. My father did work very hard to provide me with the best life that he thought he could, albeit being emotionally abusive throughout my entire childhood. In my sister's mind, I always had more than her and that was why I was able to attend college, nurture a career, and maintain a comfortable lifestyle. The problem is that I didn't have more opportunity, or any advantage over her. We both made different decisions which took our lives in very different directions.

Travis had already been exposed to the dysfunction of my father's family, when Angela and I had our run-in during the summer. Now, he was going to see what my mother and sister had to offer. I would've been nervous, if I hadn't truly believed that Travis was the one for me. He might as well had seen all of me, especially the bad, so he could understand me completely. Travis was well aware of my story, but he needed to witness it to have a true understanding. As I imagined what my family must have looked like in his eyes, I realized just how blessed I was to have him in my life.

Dinner went well. My mother and father did most of the talking, reminiscing about their courtship and the demise which quickly followed. I couldn't help but imagine what would have become of them had they stayed together. I also wondered what made them give up so easily. It appeared that they actually liked each other. They were obviously not going to get back together but they did have that personal chemistry that makes a couple seem compatible, at least on the surface. So, where did it all go wrong and would I make the same mistakes that they had? The last thing I wanted to do was end up alone, like the both of them. I was scared at just the thought of it being unavoidable. They never divorced, and while my mother dated women afterward, my father remained single. Hopefully, I hadn't inherited all of their dysfunction and if I had, I prayed that I was still enough of my own person to be able to overcome it.

All in all, I was proud of the work that I was doing for myself and my family. In the past, it seemed as if my mother had no intention of making any effort to build a relationship that would require her to go out of her way. Maybe this was her attempt to show me otherwise. This moment could be the first moment that we needed to start building momentum.

When the night ended, my mother and sister both put on their sad faces. They have this look that they usually give when they want someone to feel sorry for them. It's a helpless look that makes you feel like they are the saddest people you've ever met. It might have worked on a stranger but I had seen it all too many times before. I saw it every time that I left Virginia after visiting my mother. It was the face of a victim but there were no victims in this family of ours. There were opportunities for us to be close, but we all chose a different path each time. As a family, we simply did not value or see necessity in being a unit, and that may have been the only common bond that we shared. If we were victims, we were the victims of our own choices.

Seeing my father with my mother further humanized him to me. Seeing my mother and sister made them seem like sad and somewhat pitiful beings. Apparently, I hadn't developed the sympathy for them that I had recently developed for my father. Never had I doubted that my father would've been there for me when I really needed him and I couldn't say the same about my mother. I had definitely made some progress with my father. Thinking about all of our progress heightened my nervousness about telling him about our engagement. I decided that I would tell him right before we left, so that we could hop on the road as soon as we got done.

The next morning, Travis and I packed up the car and were literally on our way to the interstate when I decided to swing by and drop the gay marriage bomb on my father. I gave him a call and told him that we were going to stop by and see him one last time before we hit the road back to St. Louis. Not only was I going to say goodbye, but I was going to come clean about our engagement.

We took him to breakfast at the Colonial

Diner, his favorite hangout. He went there every morning for coffee and a three-dollar egg breakfast. I figured it couldn't hurt to tell him on a full stomach. As we drove him home, I became extremely nervous about how he was going to react. I didn't necessarily care whether he approved or not, I was more concerned with how it was going to affect our relationship and all the work that we had done. I was afraid that if he didn't approve, it would send us back into the dark place that we had been moving away from for so long. Travis was going to be my husband, and nothing was going to change that. All I wanted was for my father to know, and hopefully give us his blessing.

I remembered the times that he called me faggots and ridiculed my feminine ways. As usual, I asked myself questions. Had his religious faith made him more homophobic or would he be full of love as he was now aware of GOD's love? You can never anticipate how religion will change a person. For some, they become judgmental, self-righteous, and subscribe to the rules and norms set forth by a church. Others begin to understand the spiritual aspect, receive GOD's unconditional love, and then spread it to others. I was hoping that he had embraced the latter. I didn't want him to reject me, but more importantly, I wanted to know that he truly understood how good GOD's love was and how powerful it was to love others. If he was able to love and accept me, now, after so many years of homophobia and verbal abuse, that would mean that he had truly grown and he was in GOD's hands.

CHAPTER FIVE: GOD BLESS AMERICA

Angela knew about the engagement since Christmas and that meant the rest of the family knew shortly afterward. Angela was known for spreading a lot of information in a short period of time. I assumed that they all kept it a secret from my father. It was seven days into the new year and he hadn't made any mention of it. I also assumed that they probably felt the same way that I did about telling him. No one wanted to be the bearer of this news. I didn't have a choice though, and it was my responsibility. He was my father and it was my wedding. I had to be the man that I claimed that I was and tell him to his face and not over the phone.

The anticipation of telling was harder than actually telling him. Isn't it always like that? The words just seemed to slip out of my mouth in the middle of a random conversation. "I don't know when the best time for me to tell you this, but Travis and I getting married," I said. That was it. There was nothing else for me to say. All I could do was brace myself for his response. His face would indicate what was going to come out of his mouth. His eyes would either buck in disbelief or he was going to place his hand over his eyes and snicker. That's what he did when he was presented with surprises. If he was upset, his laughter would be followed by ridicule and then insults, delivered in the calmest and most demeaning tone.

He did neither this time. He didn't smile but he didn't frown. Instead he expressed what I considered to be a look of content and relief. I hadn't anticipated this look nor had I ever seen this look before in my life.

Maybe he gets it, I thought to myself. Maybe he actually gets it! When he opened his mouth, I was unprepared to receive his complete and unwavering approval! Honestly, I would've been content with his tolerance but he went further than that. He applauded Travis for coming into my life and commended the changes that he saw in me as a result. I was blown away by his acceptance of our love and his sincere blessing. I almost veered off the road.

He went on to tell Travis that he loved him because he loved me and that he was happy to have another son. Never in a million years did I expect it to go this well. Just when I thought that I couldn't be more shocked, he kept talking and it was all very positive. "Be proud and stand strong in your love and ignore what the haters will say, especially the haters in the church," he advised us. "The devil is using the church to divide us and turn us against each other, and that's not what GOD wants," he warned.

That was all that we needed to hear as we brought our excursion to a close. Both missions were accomplished and exceeded our expectations. Seeing New York wasn't planned by us but the inspiration that it gave me let me know that the universe had planned it for me. The trip to New York reminded me of the part in *The Alchemist* when the main character, only referred to as the boy, met up with a caravan of hundreds of people. Although there was so much going on in the caravan, when they crossed the desert, everyone was silent. In that silence, the boy was able to listen to the forces of nature, mainly the wind. That wind made him think of the winds that had crossed his face on previous occasions. He thought of all his experiences and how they could be connected to the fulfillment of his destiny.

My experience in New York City had put me in the same mindset as the boy in *The Alchemist*. As busy and as vibrant as the city was, I was able to hear the universe speak over all of it. The universe reminded me of who I was and who I had always dreamed of being. All at once, my past, present, and future were all moving into alignment.

Travis and I hit the highway in pretty good spirits. My father's blessing was another confirmation from the universe that we were meant to be together and that we were heading in the right direction. For someone like my father to express his acceptance as well as truly bless our union meant a lot. It was the largest step that my father had ever taken in our relationship. The things that he said to us were things that I had said and thought before. We knew GOD in the same way.

The drive back to St. Louis was somewhat melancholy. It was the first of many lasts that were on the horizon for us. This was the last time that a trip to St. Louis would be a trip home. Once we moved to Phoenix, a trip to St. Louis would be a trip out of town. It was also the last time that I would be seeing parts of America for a long time, if not the very last time. There was a slim chance to none, that I would ever drive through the mountains of Pennsylvania or see the farmland of Ohio.

In my early twenties, I used to drive to New Jersey more frequently and traveling those same roads brought back memories. Those twenty-something hour road trips alone gave me plenty of time to think and I thought about plenty during that time to myself. It was some of the only time that I had to be still and confront many of my issues. Something about the physical journey was reinvigorating to me. As I drove, I would be forced to be with myself and I couldn't distract myself from what was on my mind. When I took those trips, I always felt refreshed when I got back home to St. Louis. The older I got, the road lost much of its charm and my financial situation afforded me the luxury of airline tickets. After getting engaged, dealing with my father's illness, and essentially quitting my job, a good old road trip to New Jersey was both nostalgic and therapeutic, as it always had been.

When we got back to St. Louis, we undertook dismantling our lives there. There was so much work to be done, but we knew that if we did it right, we would never have to do it again. We were blessed to be able to afford whatever we needed to make our transition a smooth one.

As I packed my life away into boxes, it all seemed surreal. St. Louis was a safe place for me for so long that it seemed like I would never actually leave. It was the first place that I established my own home and actually felt at home. New Jersey is where I grew up but I never felt that I belonged or connected with the people there.

St. Louis was where I grew into myself, learned to love myself, and achieved so much more than anyone had ever expected of me. I conquered being a fish out of water to establish friendships, a career, and more recently, a loving relationship. Teaching made me a member of the community and forced me to immerse myself in the cultures of the families that I served. With all that being said, I still knew that it was time for me to go and blossom elsewhere.

St. Louis was full of a lot of painful memories for me and the city had become more of a dark place for me in recent months. Between the constant crime and working with families in poverty, I felt it was a matter of time before something would hit close to home. There was also something almost magical about Arizona that St. Louis just couldn't compete with.

The thought of having a going away party crossed my mind but it never gained any traction. The closer that we got to our move date, we just wanted to get out. At times, it seemed as if we were escaping or running away. The prospects that lied ahead for Travis and I excited me to the point that I was almost anxious. When I thought about staying, only negative thoughts entered my mind. I had to check those thoughts to prevent from attracting a negative energy toward our move. Sometimes, we think we are getting away from something but instead we take it with us by focusing on it so much.

The night before we left, we visited with family and friends but only for a short amount of time. Most of the day was spent packing boxes and loading the moving truck. We had completely underestimated how much work it was going to take to move our things from the second floor using an elevator. By the time the sun went down, we were both smelly, tired, and irritable. Not to mention, we must have argued at least three times that day. It was one of the most stressful days that I can remember and we weren't even finished completely at the end of that day. There were still more items that needed to be loaded the next morning.

We packed boxes and did our best to squeeze them into our packed moving truck well into the night. It was so overwhelming that there were quite a few moments when I almost broke down and cried. Nothing came out though, I was so tired that I couldn't even shed a tear. There seemed to be more trash than anything, which only contributed to additional trips up and down the elevator. After going back and forth and up and down, in repeated cycles, everything was gone.

At the end of the night we laid our tired and aching bodies on the hardwood floor. The only comfort was the three couch cushions that hadn't been thrown out with the couch. The entire apartment was empty and it was becoming a reality that there was no turning back at this point. My body ached so bad and my mind raced with thoughts of the long drive that was ahead of us. To think, we had actually contemplated leaving that night when we had packed up the truck. It must have been our eagerness to leave that made us think that we could hop on the road and go after all of that. We opted to take showers and stay just one more night. The hot shower that I took that night will remain one of my best uses of hot water ever.

January 16, move out day, was a damp and rainy morning in St. Louis. We woke up, still sore, and bid farewell to our apartment. I hadn't lived in that apartment as long as Travis had but I was just as emotional as he was about leaving. It was the first home that we had made together and the home where we spent our first holidays. Travis and I fell in love in that apartment and when we were dating, we spent many nights there watching movies and having dinners.

As we pulled out of our apartment complex for the last time, the weight of my years in St. Louis felt like it was lifted from my shoulders. The circumstances surrounding my move there and the subsequent struggles that followed would be behind me spiritually and now physically. My body ached and the cold, damp weather made me want to crawl into bed but I was energized by what was ahead of me.

Travis drove the moving truck with his car dollied to the back. I followed behind him as a buffer to the traffic behind us and to make sure that everything was safe on the back end of the truck. An air of nostalgia swept through as we rode past personal landmarks like the exit to a friend's house, the Six Flags theme park, or businesses where I interviewed for jobs and never got hired. I remembered all that I had went through while I was finding my way in a strange place that became my home.

We crossed the state line into Kansas and then again into Oklahoma. I had never been to Kansas, Oklahoma, or any of the states that I would see on my journey to my new home. I figured I wouldn't return to these parts again anytime soon, possibly never, especially not driving in a car. It was a once in a lifetime drive for me. Driving through the plains and prairies, the nerd in me thought of the pioneers who moved west in search for a better life. That was the spirit that motivated Travis and I also. Right before my eyes were parts of America that I had only seen in books. I thought about the people who would never see what I saw or even think it was possible. Not very long ago, I was one of those people but here I was, seeing more, expanding my horizons.

Thirteen hours later, we arrived in Amarillo, Texas. It was our designated halfway mark from St. Louis to Phoenix. The rest stop came just in time as the Red Bulls had lost their effect somewhere near Oklahoma City. My left leg was in excruciating pain from driving for the first thirteen hours of the trip. I was still exhausted from the night before and the next day we would drive the remaining ten hours. The bed at our two-star hotel felt like the best bed in a five-star hotel. I gave all the glory to GOD for giving whoever invented bedding the idea and grace to invent it.

The next morning, we headed out for the conclusion of our trip. The first state we entered was the beautiful state of New Mexico. The Welcome to New Mexico sign and the license plates read "The Land of Enchantment." The phrase couldn't have been more appropriate. I was never more enchanted by landscape nor had I ever even been interested. New Mexico was the most breathtaking and beautiful place I had ever seen. We were mystified as we drove up into snow-covered mountains then down into the picturesque desert. Why didn't everyone come here to see this? All that I could think about was how many other things in life were left for me to see. What else was I missing out on and why was I living with such a confined world view? GOD had indeed blessed America, and it was a blessing to see his amazing creations.

Those 10 remaining hours turned into fourteen hours as we maneuvered our moving truck through the beautiful, yet intimidating mountains in Northern Arizona. As day gave way to night, we found ourselves out of the mountains and in the darkness of the uninhabited desert. After hours in the dark, the city lights of Phoenix ascended out of the desert night, like an oasis. When we finally arrived in town, it was too late to move in, so we waited out the night in a shabby motel on the west side of town.

The next morning, we moved into our new apartment, situated just in front of the McDowell Mountains. It was the most beautiful location that I had ever called home. The weather was beautiful and it felt like spring in January, sometimes summer. When I say summer, I am referring to the summers in St. Louis or New Jersey. The Phoenix summer was no comparison to any of the summers that I had experienced before. The Phoenix winter felt like a St. Louis summer to me, so you can imagine what the actual summer in Phoenix feels like.

After we settled in, Travis and I worked to adjust to living a life that would only include the two of us. There was no one that we could turn to for help, if we needed it, and nowhere to go to escape from one another. It was only the two of us now, in a place neither of us had any knowledge of. We became more than lovers at this point. Our lives depended on one another, not because we were engaged but we were all that each other had. More than just our location had changed. We were starting our entire lives over, from scratch.

I hadn't worked on my *From Scratch* project anymore since the day I thought of it, after leaving New York. I didn't have much time to since then, preparing for such a big move. When I got time to work on it again, I wanted to add our move to Arizona as another layer to develop. *From Scratch* would pay tribute to where I came from and chronicle my journey to where I was headed.

There was a beauty in my life and a struggle that I believed so many others could relate to. From those years of struggle, I became a better person but I wasn't able to recognize it until I was in a place in life where it was safe to look back. Don't look back until you are sure that looking back will not hinder you from looking forward.

The biggest mistake we can make is to keep looking back, bringing up old pain, and keep ourselves back there in that pain.

It's been said that hindsight is 20/20 vision and 20/20 vision is exactly what I had once I embraced the laws of attraction. I recognized what I could've done differently and how things would've turned out differently had I known about the laws of attraction all of my life.

The move to Phoenix and the fresh start was reinvigorating and inspiring. For weeks, I didn't do much more than soak in the beauty of the environment. I never knew how much I could appreciate nature. Nature shows us what is really valuable, if we are still enough to see it. The power of GOD is right in front of us, every second of the day, once we remove the distractions of man. GOD was everywhere in the amazing mountains, blue skies, and vast canyons. There is a beauty in the Southwest that you cannot understand until you see it for yourself. Just breathing felt easier in Arizona.

It was the first time in my life that I made no attempts to do anything more than what I was doing at the very moment. I was being still, and I was doing a much better job than I ever had. As the days passed, I recognized that the life I had lived was not going to be it for me. There was more in store for me. Being away from my stressful job and taking time to myself was something that took getting used to but it paid off quickly. My body rejuvenated itself and the nature that was around me created a clarity inside me that is incomparable to anything else.

It seemed as though I was quickly becoming a hippy, minus the drugs. As I moved towards hippiedom, I became a nicer, more gentle person. I was so in love with life and everything that my creator had in store for me or what I would create for myself. My alignment with the universe was more perfect than it had ever been.

After a month or so of being still, I decided to put myself back out there in the job market. It couldn't hurt to look and see what was out there, or could it? Although I knew deep down inside that I didn't want to work in education, it seemed like it couldn't hurt to find a job that would utilize the wonderful resume that I had. In truth, I was having a hard time letting go, which meant I wouldn't be able to grasp for new things. I felt like I would be wasting all of my years of experience and all of my education.

What I didn't know at the time, is that any form of preparation is never wasted. Whatever we learn and experience is put to good use in the ordering of our steps. While our preparation may not be used for how it appears it should be intended, such as for a career, it always comes into use. Even if the experience happens just for the sake of the experience itself. Everything that we experience is part of a larger, holistic experience and contributes to the greater good within us in some way. No part of our life is wasted living.

None of the interviews that I went on were successful and deep down inside I didn't really want any of the jobs that I had interviewed for. They would all have required me to make a full-time commitment and would've put me right back in the same position that I was trying to get away from. My focus would no longer be on my art or the desires of my true self. My focus would be on a job, a paycheck and helping others. Helping others is a good thing but it wasn't what I had set my sights on. Call me selfish if you want but I was only concerned with aligning myself with my true self.

What I was doing was engaging in the most counterproductive and self-injurious process. I was putting myself in a position to be rejected because I was listening to those little voices of doubt way in the back of my mind. The more I listened to them, the larger they became until they eventually became my prominent thought. I did it to myself entirely. I was well aware of how the laws of attraction and the universe respond to our thinking, yet I tried to test them and in the process subjected myself to my old way of thinking.

The interviews were my attempts at testing the universe to see if it would lead me astray from the path that I wanted to go on. It didn't. As far as I had come in my life, I still had residue of the negative experiences and energy. I wasn't completely out of the woods yet.

So what prompted me to listen to those negative voices again? As much as I was in love with Arizona and my new life, the unfamiliarity of it all was unnerving at times. So much change occurred in such a short time that I subconsciously longed for some familiarity. The most familiar thing I could grasp was doubt and negativity.

This was the first time in years that I was not working and my entire identity was in a compromising position. I prided myself on my work ethic and my educational accomplishments. It was who I was, more importantly, it was my victory story. I had been put down so much that I wanted to prove myself to the world, and I did just that by graduating from college and getting a good job. Who was I going to be now? What would people say about me now? While it didn't matter to me, I didn't want anyone to have any ammunition to use against me. Not working could be used against me as ammunition, especially by my family. As far as we had come to mend fences and rebuild a relationship, I still felt in my heart that they couldn't wait to see me in a position where they could tear me back down. I wasn't out of the woods with that family situation either.

There was a piece of me who felt like I had to prove something about my move. I wanted my former co-workers, especially my former principal, to see me with a good job, better than the one that I had left. I wanted my family to see me living the most ideal life that I could, one that they would be proud of. More importantly, I wanted to continue to live a life that wouldn't make me susceptible to anyone's criticism.

The rejection from job interviews left me frustrated and even a little discouraged, but I knew in my gut that I was being rejected because I was meant to stay on the path to becoming a writer. The universe, through disappointment, was keeping me aligned with my destiny. Still, the thought of someone being able to ridicule me for not working bothered me. I knew that it would be a matter of time before someone would comment on me not having a job. Unfortunately, I had been programmed to believe that if you didn't work a job, you weren't of much value to the world. No one ever told me that I could be my own boss or reach for any goal that I had.

I was raised to think that you *had* to have a job and your priority was to keep your job. You were supposed to go to work and pay bills. If you didn't, then you were some kind of weird, dream-chasing, slacker trying to get over on the system. My mother didn't work and she was constantly degraded and devalued as a human being by my father and his family. They didn't believe in dreams or goals, and they definitely wouldn't believe in my dreams or goals. The entire time that I went to college, no one actually believed that I was going to graduate. My Aunt Etta even called me to persuade me to join the army, saying that I was wasting my time with school.

Even though we had reconciled, I still knew that I couldn't trust them with my hopes and aspirations. They would ridicule them if they knew what they were. The relationships that I had redeveloped with them only blossomed because I devalued their position in my life. I was able to embrace them because I know longer cared about their opinion, their ideas, or really anything that they had to say. They became more and more irrelevant to me as

I grew more and more self-aware. I could be in their presence and even enjoy them because of the irrelevance they had in my life.

It was only because of my father's illness that I was having more frequent dealings with them. Before he became ill, I really only saw them on special occasions. My gut told me to keep a safe distance from them but the more time I spent time with them I actually felt myself starting to care about them again. It was another one of those changes that I attributed to being in love. I let my walls down for Travis and it paid off, so I was less guarded than ever before. Before I met Travis, my walls were up to the world. I didn't realize that you could leave your walls up for some people and let them down for others. Travis was also all for me nurturing positive relationships with them. He encouraged me to forgive and give them another chance because it would make me a better person.

So, why was I so worried about them bad mouthing me, when it hadn't happened yet? Why did I even think that they would do something like that? Everything that I had buried years before was resurfacing. First, my dreams had resurfaced and my nightmares were also resurfacing. I never trusted them, couldn't trust them, and didn't trust them. That was why I felt they were waiting around for something to say about me. For my *From Scratch* project, I wanted to look back while moving forward at the same time. That was exactly what I was doing and it was a little bit more than I had bargained for. Was I really ready for this?

CHAPTER SIX: TURN FOR THE WORSE

Travis started his new job the first week in February, and after that I was home alone for most of the day. For the most part, I enjoyed the free time that I had. I had a little bit of guilt, but not much, about leaving my students behind in St. Louis. When I decided to leave my job, I knew there would be moments where I felt torn because I had been teaching for so long. Surprisingly, I didn't really think about it very much. Instead, I started nurturing more and more of the creative energy that was inside of me. I had only jotted down notes about my *From Scratch* project up until that point and I was ready to dig deeper into the concept.

My friends had been telling me to write for years, whenever I shared stories with them about my love life or even the things I went through at work. I was never able to just sit down and actually do it though. With work and school, I was always obligated to do something other than write. When I would finish writing papers or grading papers, I didn't want to do anything.

Now that I had the time to write, I knew that I had to take advantage of the opportunity. It felt like it was my time. I thought of other things that I wanted to do to maximize all this time that I now had to do whatever I wanted. I came up with an idea that I would apply my *From Scratch* concept across multiple media platforms. I wanted to express myself in many ways. I would start with a podcast and a documentary series, that I could upload online.

Building my own media platforms became my job. If I approached it as my job, I would not revert back to my old way of thinking and feel that I needed to look for a job. Travis was adamant about me getting to work on my creative aspirations. He insisted that we hadn't moved across the country to continue to live the way that we had lived in St. Louis. It was the first time that I was fully supported and free to immerse myself in my dreams. The only problem I had was determining where to start.

Every idea excited me and so many thoughts flooded my head that I didn't know how to focus. I needed to be still. My mind was all over the place and I kept thinking about the possible outcomes instead of living in the moment. I knew what I wanted the end result to be for all of my ideas but couldn't get going. Having a vision and a big picture is a good thing, but it means nothing if you can't follow the steps to get to it.

My father and I were talking every day or every other day and I planned to start visiting him once a month. Never would I have predicted that we would make it to that point, but we were in a good place. My father and I started speaking about more personal topics, such as the things I wanted to do with my writing, my decision to stop teaching, and even my relationship with my mother. I started to feel like I was a son who had a father he could talk to and get advice from.

Travis and I traveled to Las Vegas and Los Angeles and each visit I made sure that I picked out souvenirs for my father, something that I hadn't considered before. Whenever we went places, I wished that he could experience what I was experiencing because I was so happy. He told me that he couldn't wait to come visit us in Phoenix. He said he heard such great things from people from Jersey who went to Arizona for drug rehabilitation.

My father also encouraged me to work on my relationship with my mother. As a kid, he had always talked about her terribly, just as Angela and his mother had. We discussed her before and he had encouraged reconciliation in the past, but this time he emphasized how good it would be for me.

Not many of our family members understood the relationship that my father and I had and it seemed as if they placed much of the blame for its failure on me, or at least in recent years. For a long time, I believed that I suffered from some type of emotional malfunction because I didn't feel much of anything toward him. There weren't any fond memories or stories that I could share like others would about their father. I never missed him or admired much about him. Truthfully, he was always a person that I tried to avoid because I didn't really want to be around him.

Most of our belief systems tell us that If you're related to someone, you are required to tell them you love them and love is given or received by default. Whether there is proof of actual love is unnecessary, the notion that you are loved is evidenced by the simple assertion that you are told. But shouldn't you feel that someone loves you, even if they don't say it? And if they do say they love you, shouldn't you genuinely believe them and feel that love? I was confused about whether my father loved me but growing up I was sure that I didn't love him.

The older I got I found myself pitying him but it still wasn't love. I felt bad for the life that he chose to live and wished he could have experienced some happiness and peace in his life. When he got sick, I did what I thought was right. I had compassion for him because he was in such a fragile state. We had gotten so far that I felt horrible for still not feeling that love I was supposed to feel. I had to be honest with myself though, I felt obligated, and didn't necessarily act out of love.

On February 27, 2016, a Saturday evening, I was informed that my father's health had suddenly taken a turn for the worse. Angela called and said that my father had suffered a seizure, hit his head, and had blood on his brain. She said that the doctors had all but given up on him, mainly because he had so many afflictions going on in addition to the head injury. Angela sobbed and asked me when I was going to make it to town. Everything was all so sudden and shocking, that I wasn't really sure what I was hearing. Even when you know someone is sick, you're still never prepared for such a sudden turn for the worse.

Regardless of our family history, I believed that this was a time when we were all supposed to look past our differences and come together. At least that's what people say. I did not necessarily believe in that but I figured it couldn't hurt to try and believe it. I had never dealt with the death of someone so close, so I was struggling with my thoughts and feelings about it. I had been planning to visit my father in the near future but not as soon as this. I simply wasn't ready to uproot the roots that I had just began to lay in Phoenix.

My heart wasn't being tugged at the way I felt it should have been and I felt guilty. My father and his health concerned me but it wasn't my first priority. I felt bad about that also. There was still some residue of an irreparable rift. It wasn't a rift that created anger or resentment, it was a rift that prevented us from being like other fathers and sons. What made the rift irreparable was the fact that it didn't even bother me that it was there. There were moments during his illness where I had amazing moments of clarity about him but none were strong enough to completely bridge the gap between us.

I knew what I was supposed to do but it wasn't what I really wanted to do. I wanted to stay in Phoenix. I also wanted to have compassion for my father and be by his side, but it would require dealing with more than just him. Dealing with the family, negativity was inevitable, and my life was pretty much perfect in Phoenix. The beautiful geography, my developing sense of peace, and my handsome fiancé were all in Phoenix. It was becoming my home and had only given me reason to believe that everything in my life was going to get better. What felt right for me was to continue to live my life, enjoy my new home, and continue to do the work that I was doing to better my own life.

I also wasn't prepared to leave Travis behind. Since our first Christmas, we hadn't spent a day apart. He was unable to take off work for the first 90 days at his new job, so he wouldn't be able to accompany me. If I had to go to Jersey, I would have to do it alone. We were starting a new life, so it was important for Travis to keep his job, especially since I didn't have one. This was going to be the first time since being together that we would be apart and I would have to travel alone. We never travelled apart, no matter what the costs were.

The thought of leaving Travis behind in Phoenix made my stomach turn. If we still lived in St. Louis, where he has family and friends, it wouldn't have been as devastating. We didn't know a soul in Phoenix, or even how to get around yet. He had also been my emotional support as I dealt with my father's illness and my conflicted emotions. I wasn't sure how I would deal with it all without him by my side. Nevertheless, I felt pressured to get there quickly, so I booked a flight out to Philadelphia for the very next morning.

The next morning, I left for Jersey without an anticipated return date. I didn't know how long I would be gone or what was going to happen while I was there. The night before, I held Travis close to me and I cried thinking about being apart from. This man meant so much to me and after waiting for so long to find him, I didn't want to spend a day of my life without him, for any reason. I knew we would be stronger when we came out on the other side of being apart but I still didn't want to have to be apart.

On our way to the airport, we sat in silence, gripping each other's hands. We didn't say much, but our demeanor spoke volumes. The closer we got to the airport, the more difficult it was for Travis to fight back his tears. He broke down in tears as we pulled into the entrance to the terminal. He clenched his fists and sounded like he was beginning to hyperventilate. His throat sounded like it was closing up as he told me that he loved me. His pain was visible and I was devastated. I felt like my stomach was on fire and that I could pass out at any moment.

I didn't know that I was capable of feeling that way. In the same breath, there was something very familiar about it. I couldn't remember the last time I longed for anyone or missed someone but I could pinpoint exactly when I had felt this pain before. It was the same pain that I used to have when I would leave my visits with my mother. The pain felt like all love have been removed and replaced with nothing but emptiness.

Long before my mother and I became estranged, I loved her with all of my heart, as most children do. When I would have to leave her and return to my father's custody, it caused me unbearable pain. It never dulled, no matter how many times it happened. It stayed for days and sometimes weeks. At some point, when I was around 11 or 12, she stopped sending for me, which is when our relationship began to disintegrate. I think that was when I gave up on love the first time. Afterwards I was immune to most of my emotions, with the exception of anger.

That trip to the airport exposed me to longing for a person for the first time since I could remember. It was the first time since childhood that I felt truly vulnerable. As an adult, I took pride in being a fighter and a force of one. The only emotion I expressed or felt usually was anger. As I walked through the airport, all of the emotions that I thought were long gone resurfaced. My heart was breaking and its pieces were laying in my gut. Now I understood why people were always in the airport crying. I thought about Travis and all my pain went away. His pain took me over. I was the one who took care of him. What was he going to do all alone in a new city? Who would feed him? Love him? Take care of him?

My thoughts spiraled out of my control. What if my plane crashed? What if Travis got hurt while I was away? I knew better than to keep engaging in that kind of thinking, but it's difficult to reign in out-of-control thoughts, when your emotions are just as out of control. Hence, people say things they really don't intend to say when they become angry or sad.

All I wanted to do was leave out the airport and return back home with Travis. Just like when I was a child and all I wanted was my mother and nothing else. The past and the present were colliding again. My fiancé and I were hopelessly codependent, I know. It didn't matter to me how pathetic or unhealthy someone else may have deemed our codependency. Loving Travis felt like it was one area of my life where I wasn't going to compromise or question any of my thoughts or feelings. I had been independent long enough, I wanted to be dependent.

The flight to Philadelphia was much quicker than expected. If you visit Southern New Jersey, Philadelphia International is the closest airport to fly in to. It was the first time that I had flew there from Phoenix, but it didn't seem much longer than my flights from St. Louis. The pilot said he caught a good headwind, whatever that means, and we landed ahead of schedule. It was like *everything* was happening entirely too fast.

I landed in Philadelphia and headed straight to the intensive care unit. The hospital was also in Philadelphia, about 15 minutes from the airport. The hospital he was in had a much better reputation than the local hospital in Jersey. It was also the same hospital that he spent a year in after his accident when he was 17. He also went there on a regular basis for chemotherapy treatments. My grandmother had died in the local hospital and the townspeople regularly made jokes that the local hospital was where folks went to die.

Camille picked me up from the airport on her way

to the hospital to visit. Angela was there with Irene and her daughter Mya. For some reason, my father had grown fond of Mya. I really didn't care for her, not even a little bit. Mya and my father had grown very close in recent years, since Mya and Irene moved back to New Jersey from St. Louis. Back in the day, Irene left New Jersey with her four children and moved to St. Louis for twenty something years. She had two sons and two daughters, all of whom were much older than the rest of the grandchildren. Mya was always annoying to me as a kid and even though she was 7 years older than me, I always viewed her as immature. Mya also liked to pry, so I limited conversations with her as much as possible.

My father laid there in a hospital bed in the most helpless state, with tubes coming from everywhere. There was nothing about him that was recognizable, and nothing appeared to be promising. I felt terrible. I wasn't necessarily distraught because I was losing my father, but more because it was my fellow man in a state of struggle and pain.

Irene and Angela brought me up to speed on the options that they had been presented by the doctors. Since I was his only child, all the pressure was on me to make a decision about the next steps in his treatment. It almost felt like the buck was being passed to me, not because I was his son, but because nobody felt comfortable with making such a tough decision. I didn't blame them. I would've passed the buck too, if I could have. At that moment, I thought about how it would've been nice to have a brother or sister around, someone to go through this with.

About an hour after I arrived, a doctor entered the room and immediately began discussing "quality of life" and resuscitation. I was completely flustered with the responsibility that I had walked into. How is one supposed to respond when the life or death of another human being, your parent at that, is dependent upon the words that come out of your mouth? Nothing could have prepared me for this kind of pressure. If he was going to die, I had to come to terms and quickly. If he was going to live, I would have to step up and rearrange my entire life to care for him.

Over the next couple days, I spent my time by my father's hospital bed, waiting on something to change. The doctors wanted to take him off life support and looked to me to give them the go ahead. They continued to comment about "quality of life" and basically urged us to let him go. My father couldn't talk and spent most of the time unconscious. One time he awoke and glared at me. I couldn't determine if the glare was telling me to save his life or let him go. I wondered if he thought I was going to use the opportunity to get back at him for all that he had done. I would never do that, but what if he was thinking that?

Spending so much time around family reminded me of all the emptiness I felt as a child. Even as my father laid there dying, I couldn't help but want to get back to Travis. All I wanted to do was get back to my new life, get back to my future, get back to love. What a piece of shit I was, I thought to myself. How does a person end up like me? I had to be the coldest person on Earth.

Just a few days in New Jersey reminded me of why I never moved back. Even though I had been back to visit, it was always for a special occasion. It was hard adjusting to being around the family on a constant basis. There was no hotel room for me to go to and no car that I could hop in and visit friends or cross the bridge and go to Philly. I was surrounded by family day and night. Within a matter of days, I was drinking every night, and going to bed as early as I could. All I wanted was to be back with Travis, and away from them.

When I left town for St. Louis, almost 15 years prior, something permanent and irreversible happened to whatever relationship that any of us had. No matter how much we got along, there was always going to be a rift in my relationship with this family. That was evident during the days that we spent together. Travis and I talked as much as possible on the phone and the rest of my time was spent at the hospital. I got along with the family while I was there but my heart lived somewhere else.

Sleeping on Angela's couch reminded me of all the times that I spent the night at her house as a child. There was an uncomfortable energy that reminded me of how uncomfortable I was when I was younger. Angela's house was always a hot spot for company and gossip. It didn't matter what day of the week it was, there was always a revolving door of friends and locals. Most of them came to drink, all of them came to gossip. Perhaps, all that gossiping contributed to some of the uncomfortable energy in the house. Bottom line is, Angela's house was not my home, and no matter how hard you try to make yourself at home, home is truly where your heart is.

At some point, all of the family dynamics had changed also. The last time I checked, Mya was one of Angela's least favorite people. Angela and Irene had never been close, and because of that, Mya never really cared for Angela either. Angela and Etta were close in age and also appeared to have a closer relationship. Irene was closer to my father in age and was never fond of her baby sister Angela. That was one of the first things Irene shared with me when I moved to St. Louis. Irene had also tried to indoctrinate her kids with not so positive ideas about both Angela and my grandmother. Mya was loyal to her mother and kept her distance from Angela. Over the years, when they did try to interact, Mya and Angela would always end up fighting.

Irene's other daughter, Kyle didn't go for the indoctrination and remained loyal to Angela and my grandmother. Kyle grew even closer to Angela when she cut ties with Irene and Mya. She hadn't spoken to either of them in many years, but called Angela a few times a week. Kyle and Angela's closeness irritated Irene and Mya for many years, but I guess they found a way to move past everything. I didn't get the memo, but I noticed that Irene and Mya were stopping by Angela's house on a daily basis to partake in the drinking, and of course the gossip.

When my grandmother was alive, Angela wouldn't have welcomed Irene or Mya to her house. My grandmother made it clear that she didn't care for either of them and because of that, Angela didn't like them either. It was like team sports when my grandmother was alive. You were either on the team that she liked or the team that she didn't like. I was on the team she didn't like. When she died, things got a little better. That was when I started talking to Angela again. She didn't bother with me while my grandmother was still alive. That would've gotten her in trouble with the coach.

I guess Angela had changed her views about them, or maybe she just pretended not to like them when grandmother was alive, because she seemed to be very fond of Irene and Mya. It didn't make any sense to me or a difference, I never liked Mya or any of them for the most part.

I knew that I had to be careful around all of them because they had obviously found some common ground and I didn't know what it was. Whenever they all were getting along, it was because they were going to turn on someone, or they already had. I also couldn't predict how long they would be on good terms. They could have just been coming together for my father, or maybe they had actually gotten past all of those years of negative feelings toward each other. It was always difficult to tell what was real and it was too much at the time to try and figure out.

As shocking as it was that Angela and Mya were getting along so well, I was even more shocked at how quickly Angela turned on Mya, as if they were still enemies. Mya stopped by Angela's house a few times during the week I was staying there, and every time she left, Angela went right to work talking about her like a dog. Shay and Camille co-signed, as daughters in the family always do. I couldn't wait to put my two cents in either, but it made sense for me to. Everyone knew that I didn't like Mya.

There was some pretty good gossip out on Mya, the biggest gossip being that she was sleeping around with a married professional football player. On top of that, the man didn't know how old she really was or that she had an 18- year old son. He thought Mya was a single, young, twenty-something. I should've known then that she had some serious insecurities to deal with. Mya is 40, has an 18-year old son, and should be proud that he wouldn't even be able to tell that she was lying about her age but when you're insecure you don't even notice how good you've got it. It wasn't the first time that Mya had messed around with a married man. She dated a very famous boxer back in 90's, who was also married.

Angela was my godmother for my entire life and I had seen her behave like this time and time again. I couldn't figure out why I was so bothered now by the things that I had been used to for so long. I guess I really had changed for the better. In my heart, I knew I was a better person than I had ever been, and that must have been why the negativity bothered me when it had never bothered me before. The very same behaviors I had seen before and dismissed, looked completely different with the clarity that I had. I had grown so much that I had outgrown the shenanigans that took place in my family. Things had definitely taken a turn for the worse and I'm not only referring to my father's health.

I wasn't surprised that Angela would reveal so much gossip so freely, but I had forgotten just how fake she was. I wondered what she said about me when I left. I didn't actually wonder nor did I really care. The point is, I knew that she still couldn't be trusted with any of my business. I'm pretty sure that Mya didn't expect Angela to be sharing that interesting tidbit. I was reminded how things had always been in our family and took note. There was always talking behind each other's back and just basic cruelty towards one another. It was also proof that they hadn't all had some phenomenal change of heart. Everyone was keeping up a facade. Then came my questions. So, what else wasn't real?

CHAPTER SEVEN: SISTER ACT

As much as I couldn't stand Mya, I had to give it to her for spending so much time at the hospital with my father. Irene, Angela, and I spent the days up there and Mya came at night when she got off work. Their relationship reminded me of how my relationship used to be with Irene. When I first moved to St. Louis, Irene and I shared a friendship, and it wasn't just because she was my father's sister. Irene and I got one another as people. It seemed that Mya and my father had gotten one another in the same fashion.

Most people thought that Angela and I were the closest because I spent so much time with her growing up. We never really connected on any deep levels but we did have fun together when we were getting along. Angela liked to have a good time and that was something about her that made it easy for me to overlook a lot of the things that she did and said. I think that most of us in the family were so used to Angela's shenanigans that we gave her a pass for a lot of things. It's just the way that it was.

I couldn't preoccupy myself too much with the changing family dynamics nor was that what I was there for. My father's situation wasn't as dire as it was first presented to me but things were still not good. I wanted him to get to some point of stabilization, so that I could get back home. Travis and I spoke daily and each day it was hard to hang up without knowing when I was going to get back home. Something was off in New Jersey and I couldn't point my finger on it. My energy simply didn't align with the energy that was there. Just the idea of not knowing how long I would have to stay there was becoming harder for me to handle each day.

The doctors presented me with the option to take my father off life support and see if he could breathe on his own. Since he had been on a ventilator for so long, there was a chance that his lungs would not work naturally without the ventilator. I'm not a doctor so I just couldn't wrap my head around why they put him on a ventilator in the first place, if it was going to inhibit his ability to breathe naturally. The doctors said that they had to put him on a ventilator because he was having too many seizures while conscious. In order to prevent those seizures, they sedated him and that required him to use a ventilator. The threat to his life at this point was not cancer, nor the blood on his brain, but now it was his inability to breathe on his own.

The tone of the conversation with the doctors wasn't what I had expected. My belief system had been influenced by idealism and too much television. They were blatantly in favor of us letting him go. I was under the impression that doctors were crusaders for human life and did whatever they could to hold onto and grasp any life that was to be lived. Yet, these doctors were much more concerned with what would be the most practical solution. They didn't express any value for his life nor did they seem to care what happened to him.

The more that I spoke with the doctors, they went on and on about what could be wrong with him and how they couldn't do this and couldn't do that for him. They painted a hopeless picture for my father and only presented us with the obstacles ahead and then the obstacles that he would face after overcoming those obstacles. Not only did he have cancer in his lungs, it had spread, and was possibly in his brain. The doctors didn't know for sure if the cancer had spread to his brain because there was a blood clot in his head that formed after he hit his head during a seizure. No one really knew what was going on, so they conceded that there was too much going on for them to be of any service.

They were the most negative and faithless group of people I had ever met. I was astonished that these were the people that so many of us trust our lives and the lives of our loved ones with. I had always been cynical about the health care system and the medicine that they gave to us, but this was too much, even for a cynic like myself. I discovered a sobering and alarming truth. Doctors are just people like you and I. They will only do so much for a person who they have no attachment to. Miracles and true recovery had to come from somewhere or someone else, somewhere or someone much greater. Miracles came from a higher power.

As I came to clarity about where his healing was going to come from and what these people were here for, I asked the doctor one simple question that redirected the entire interaction. "What *can* you do for him?" with the emphasis on the *can*. I was tired of hearing what couldn't be done. The look on the doctor's face was as if he was in unchartered territory. You would've thought that I asked him what the meaning of life was. He was out of his comfort zone. Immediately, he reverted back to how bad things were and highlighted my father's lack of chance at survival and how poor his quality of life would be if he did survive. "Yes, we understand, but what can *you* do for him?" I shot back, this time with the emphasis on the *you*. "We will pray for him and hope for the best. All I need to know is what services *you* can provide," I added. I had reached my wits end with the dark and gloomy and the focus on the negative. My thoughts needed to remain positive to attract positive energy from the universe. My goal at that point was to take the next steps, have the doctor do whatever he could do, and wait on GOD to point us in the next direction.

The doctor said he could provide him with a tracheotomy, which would give him the best chance at being able to breathe on his own later. So, that's what I asked them to do. My father received a tracheotomy and was taken off life support. There was still cancer in his lungs and nobody knew what was going on his brain. We could only take things one step at a time. I wasn't going to give into the negative thinking and energy that his doctors had brought into the room. If my father was going to die, it was because it was his time to die. It wasn't going to be because some doctor devalued his life or didn't see the point in saving a man's life who only had Medicare for insurance. My father was going to have a chance to let the universe help him and GOD carry him.

After a few days, he was off the tracheotomy and breathing completely on his own. The first step was successful. Positive momentum was building and who knew what the possibilities were. There was no point in thinking otherwise at a time like this. We all knew that his life would never be the same again, but he was still going to be here. In a few days, he was going to be moved to a rehabilitation facility. He was going to need assisted living services, but I still believed that he could make a full recovery. I didn't believe because of our healthcare system, I believed because I had my GOD and my knowledge of the laws of the universe. GOD makes miracles happen when you believe and the universe brings whatever you believe to you as fast as possible.

My father's recovery made me feel good about being there and the decision that I had made. Still, I wanted to get back home to Travis. It wasn't a good time to be around my family, even though my father was still fighting for his life. I was paying close attention to every little thing they were doing and I was more critical of them than ever. I hadn't come to terms with or understood how just weeks after Angela had my father's utilities cut off in an effort to spite him, she sat in his hospital room and cried over him. I wanted to make sense of the inconsistency, but as much as I tried to explain it away, I couldn't.

I couldn't pretend that I didn't see what was right before my eyes. Talking myself out of how I felt was not going to work anymore. My eyes didn't see as they used to.

The universe was blaring a spotlight on all that I wasn't able to see for so long. The issues from my childhood that I struggled to make sense of for much of my adult life were now beginning to make perfect sense. No matter how old or independent I was, I felt like a vulnerable and exposed child around them. The traumatic experiences of my childhood ran deep and everything that I had going on emotionally, was making it all resurface. My father, and mother, made some very big mistakes, but there were some other people involved and their participation had just as much impact on my life as my parents.

With my father stable and headed to a rehab facility, I hightailed it back to Phoenix. I didn't waste a minute, once I knew I could leave. I believed that my father was going to come back from it all, especially if he believed and thought he could come back from it. The only problem was that I wasn't sure that my father himself truly believed that it was possible.

I contemplated staying longer but I was missing Travis. Even worse was how I felt being around my family members. I would have to go back to Jersey sooner than later, but I needed to get back to my home, recover a bit, and try to reclaim my thoughts.

The flight back to Phoenix seemed like it was three times as long as the flight was to Philadelphia. I could barely contain my excitement to embrace the love of my life. Seeing my father's condition, only made me think how short our time is here, even if a lifetime. Travis was the most important person in my life and enjoying life with him was my top priority. I wanted to make sure that we cherished every moment together.

The warm Phoenix weather was a stark contrast from the snow and chill of New Jersey. The palm trees and sunlight only make you feel like you are on a never-ending vacation. Just being back there was enough to boost my spirits. Reuniting with Travis was an immediate relief and I knew we were a stronger couple from the separation. There wasn't a doubt in my mind before that Travis was the right one for me, but being apart only reinforced my feelings. Seeing him in anguish when I left showed me how deep our connection was. On the way home from the airport, we vowed then that we would never leave each other's side.

After just a few days, I forgot how bad things were for my dad. I guess I had blocked it out. Truth is, I was focused on the moments that I was living. I really wanted to completely forget about his sickness, the pending future, and all of the negativity. The icky and negative vibrations that seemed to be all over me in Jersey subsided once I left.

Travis and I discussed bringing my father out to Phoenix, since he would require long-term rehabilitation. More than ever before, I was seeing him in a different light and I wanted to help him in the best way that I could. I couldn't distinguish between whether it was love or compassion because there was such a complicated backstory. Nevertheless, I felt something. I made up my mind that I would go back to working, if I needed to take care of his medical expenses. We were in a pretty good financial spot as was but caring for a cancer patient would've required a substantial income boost.

My father continued to show tenacity in the following weeks. Things had improved to the point that he no longer needed the tracheotomy and could breathe and talk on on his own. He was well enough that we were able to resume phone conversations again. When we talked, I could hear the weakness in his voice but he still sounded like he was beginning his road to recovery. When I told him I would be working on getting him out to Phoenix, he spoke clearly and with a slight excitement and said "I may need to come out there for a long time!" Phoenix is home to an awesome cancer center, but I believed the natural beauty is where the real healing power is.

By mid-March he fully stabilized and was admitted

to a rehabilitation facility in Jersey, where he would adjust to a new lifestyle with much assistance. The writer in me was superstitious about the time of year. As a kid, I would read old literature and there were mentions of the "ides of March." I found out what it meant in my senior year of high school, when I finally asked my English teacher. I've never been superstitious but "beware of the ides of March" has always stuck with me.

Mya created a text message group that shared updates on his status. I would call to check and see how things were going but usually we all communicated through texting. There weren't many calls made, but the texts came on a daily basis. It appeared as if my father's condition was bringing us together as a family, or at least building a foundation. We didn't share group messages before or at least I wasn't included in them to know. Even though I had my reservations about remaining in contact with them, I felt it was the right thing to do.

A few weeks passed and I got a call. It wasn't a call that I wanted. The care at the rehabilitation facility was less than stellar. The level of care at the facility was not appropriate for someone in his condition. My father ended up back in intensive care at the hospital. At the hospital, he declined quicker than ever and to a worse degree than before he went to the rehabilitation facility. Tired of it all, my father had given up and declined to receive additional care. He was sent home on hospice. He was going to die very soon.

Travis went with me this time to visit my father's bedside. I couldn't imagine leaving him in Phoenix again. We had vowed to never leave each other's side and we stood by that. In my suitcase, were enough clothes to last a week and a black shirt just in case there was a funeral service. Travis could only stay for two days and then he would have to go back. Since we weren't married, he could not get time off from his job unless there was an actual funeral. That was the first time we actually discussed a wedding date. We contemplated getting married before we left, so that he could stay with me as long I needed him. I didn't even want to be there, let alone stay, but felt like I was obligated to stay because it was my father.

As soon as we landed in Philadelphia, Etta called to rush me as if my father was going to die at any minute. Travis and I went straight to Bordentown, where my father was receiving hospice care. Bordentown, New Jersey is just over an hour south of New York City, about 45 minutes from Philadelphia, and about 35 minutes from where I lived growing up in Woodbury, NJ, depending on how you drive. The house he was at belonged to my Great Aunt Diane, who herself had passed just a few months prior in November. She was 91 years old and had spent many years dealing with her own illness, but remained a symbol of longevity in our family. Irene took care of her in her final days, and assumed the same duty of taking care of my father in his final days. She was close by when my grandmother died and took care of my father when he was hospitalized as a teenager.

Aunt Diane's house was already conducive for hospice care as Aunt Diane had been receiving in-house medical care for decades. It brought back fond memories from my childhood, a contrast to many of the memories I had from my own childhood home. I spent a lot of time at Aunt Diane's house as a kid as she didn't have any children of her own. Since I was the youngest boy in the family with the family name, she treated me like I was special and always looked out for me growing up. I had the same name as her father, my great-grandfather. My grandfather wasn't named after my great-grandfather but he gave the name to his son, my father, who then gave the name to me.

Being from a much more family-oriented time, Aunt Diane saw value in names and legacies. The Huffington family had a respected name in Bordentown, especially during my grandfather and Aunt Diane's time. It is a small town, full of churchgoers, which was even smaller many years ago. Our family was full of teachers, business owners, and professionals. The family's reputation in Bordentown was markedly different than it was in Woodbury. In Woodbury, we were known for drinking and attending church maybe once a year, on Easter. Aunt Diane was the last remaining Huffington in Bordentown, so she took a lot of pride in her family's home and legacy.

Growing up, I didn't know why or how she was my aunt because I didn't really pay attention to most things. I was in my own world most of the time and as long as you were nice to me that's all that mattered. She was sweet to me as far as I could remember and I never understood why my father, grandmother, and Angela would talk about her so badly. As a kid, I wasn't wise enough to realize that they were just being mean and messy; I thought that the people they talked about were actually as messed up as they characterized them to be.

They didn't just talk about Aunt Diane, they tore everyone down, even those they called their best friends. People would literally come to visit with them, leave, and they would talk about them before they got to their cars. No one was off limits when my grandmother and Angela got together, not even children.

Most of my early years were spent listening to how horrible I was, when I wasn't listening to how terrible my mother and father were. Sometimes, they talked about Irene and Etta, and their kids too. The only people that they didn't talk about were themselves or Angela's daughters and husband. Not only did they not get talked about but Angela, Camille, Shay and Uncle Carl were projected as perfect in every way. Any fault of theirs was justified, downplayed, or abruptly moved on from. Angela and my grandmother spent hours either on the phone, or face-to-face, going on and on about how everyone in the world was living wrong or imperfect, according to their ideals.

While Angela and my grandmother always put me down, Aunt Diane always celebrated me. She spoke highly of my father as well. She would pick me up for weekends and take me to church with her. We would ride around visiting her friends, all of whom treated me like the handsome and charming boy that I was. I'll never forget when she took me to Six Flags Great Adventure for the first time and I got to ride every ride that I could fit on. While she was much older, it didn't stop her from getting on rides and pretending to enjoy them. When she couldn't hang anymore, she would watch me from a nearby bench, always smiling.

Every Christmas, Aunt Diane would drive from Bordentown to visit on the day after New Year's. Her gift would be the last gift of the holiday season. It was the last chance to get that gift that you asked for but didn't get. Her gift never turned out to be that gift that you were hoping for but just knowing that there was still hope was part of the fun. She would come just when you almost lost the holiday spirit with one last reminder of the joys of Christmas. I knew what to expect from her each year, cologne of some sort, followed by intense criticism of the gift from her niece Angela, and sister-in-law, my grandmother. Nothing that they said stopped me from thinking so highly of her.

After she passed away in November, my father and I were the only two members of the family left still carrying on the family name. Aunt Diane represented our name extremely well as evidenced by the outpouring of community support and recognition the family received at her funeral. Her service was one that uplifted and left you in an amazing space.

The preacher celebrated her life and encouraged us to continue to walk in the path that she had walked upon, a path of service, faith, and kindness. I learned things about Aunt Diane at her funeral, that I had never known before, including her work with children with disabilities and the magnitude of her faith. I was personally touched by what seemed to be our similar paths walked at two different points in time. I felt blessed to have had her in my life and I smiled inside. She was always amazing to me but I soon learned that day how amazing she was to so many others.

The preacher emphasized that Aunt Diane would've wanted us to rejoice in the fact that she was going to heaven and not cry about her leaving Earth. He got in a good word as well that day, just the way that she would've wanted it. He must have known about the family dynamic because he made sure to touch upon relationships and how we do GOD's work by loving one another. The sermon made me feel as though I should be spending more time in church. It had been a while since I actually listened to someone preach and it went a long way at the time. I had never anticipated that I would leave a funeral in good spirits and that spoke volumes as to who my Aunt Diane was.

Since Aunt Diane passed away, Irene lived in the house all by herself. Although Aunt Diane didn't die in the house her spirit still permeated the rooms, in a positive way. Perhaps it was her belongings or the memories associated with the house but I felt that she was there and always will be. There was a history in this home and in the town of Bordentown, where much of my family's legacy originated. My father spending his last moments there would be comforting for him. Knowing that he would be comforted by being there brought me more peace than I could have asked for. He was the eldest male with the Huffington name so returning to his origins seemed fitting and somewhat poetic.

My father had decided that he was ready to face the unknown, so I was accepting of the inevitable. He was going to transition on his own terms, which I know for him was easier than continuing to struggle in uncertainty. His siblings seemed much more uneasy about his transition than he or I was. I envied their attachment as I wished that I could feel the same. At times, I wondered if they were acting. If they were acting, I wished that I could act the same.

CHAPTER EIGHT: LEGACY

My father was blessed to have his sisters there for him whenever he needed them. My sister and I would never be as close as they were. It was just too late for us to bond the way that they had. My cousins were closer to me than my own sister, especially Camille and Shay, who were also my god-sisters. At times, my aunts played more of a mother role than my own mother. Angela was my godmother but I never felt comfortable being open with her because of how mean she was, especially when she talked about my mother.

Etta was always cool to me but I never really bonded with her on a deeper level growing up. I always liked her but she never tried to be a mother figure, and that made me like her more. Etta was happy just to be my aunt and didn't need to be elevated in my life. She was always good to me when we visited her as kids, and that was good enough for me. Etta always told me how smart I was as a boy, among many other compliments. She never made me feel inferior, or less than, as Angela did.

Irene was probably the aunt that I had gotten the closest to out of all of them. When I moved to St. Louis, it was because she had opened her doors. She took me in and treated me as her own, maybe better than her own, if you ask some of her children. She was the also first adult in the family that I confided in about my father and everyone in the family. Irene was the first person that I had ever met that truly understood my feelings and validated them.

We bonded over the common experiences we shared being apart of our family. She said that she was treated the exact same way as I was and that our family had operated in this dysfunction long before I was born. I could tell Irene all about what I wanted to do with my life, and she never ridiculed me. She actually believed in me, or at least led me to believe that she did.

When it came to my father, Irene understood exactly how I felt. Irene was not my grandmother's favorite and everyone knew it. That was the basis for much of Irene's dislike of Angela. Angela was the favorite and everyone also knew that. But Irene's relationship with her mother was much deeper than just feeling like she wasn't the favorite. There was a long held resentment that Irene struggled to come to terms with for years.

Many of Irene's life experiences paralleled mine. For example, we both had started over from scratch in St. Louis after leaving behind our toxic family in New Jersey. Irene and I also struggled to come to terms with abandonment issues and resentment toward our parents.

After my grandmother died in 2003, Irene was very open and upfront about how she didn't feel that she felt the way she was supposed to. Her mother's death hadn't made her anymore sympathetic or reflective about her relationship with her mother. Irene still retained the resentment toward her mother, even after she passed. She may have even been more resentful that they were unable to come to terms before her death.

Irene's resentment went back decades to before Angela and Etta were even born. She was born 10 years before them and 9 months before my father. Irene grew up in Bordentown for the early years of her life, and felt that she was abandoned by her mother. Aunt Diane was the woman whom she viewed as her mother figure, another parallel to my childhood experiences.

Of course, my grandmother had a differing account of what happened which Angela believed over Irene's. For decades, Angela and Irene had a fundamental rift in their relationship because Angela believed Irene hated their mother for no reason, and Irene felt that her mother abandoned her, didn't want her, and turned her sister against her.

Irene's daughters grew up caught in the middle.

My grandmother thought the world of Irene's oldest daughter, Kyle, and she was intensely loyal to her in return. Kyle was definitely one of my grandmother's favorites. Maybe it was because Kyle was her first grandchild. Irene only escalated the issues with her mother when she named her youngest daughter after Aunt Diane. It was symbolic of how close she was with Aunt Diane and was Irene's way of honoring her. That could've been part of the reason why my grandmother and Angela were always so critical of Aunt Diane, because of the underlying issues surrounding Irene's upbringing, living with Aunt Diane. Mya never liked the name Diane, so she always went by her middle name Mya.

Irene's daughter's ended up hating one another in the same way that Irene and Angela had hated each other for so long. They have been at odds since childhood. Irene ended up doing the very same thing that her mother had done to her to her daughters. Kyle and Irene also shared the same dysfunctional mother-daughter relationship that Irene had with her mother. Mya and Irene remain close as ever, just as Angela was with their mother. Kyle does not talk to her mother or Mya at all, just as Irene didn't communicate with my grandmother or Angela. Irene and her daughters are caught up in a generational curse that looks to continue.

Kyle has refused to even consider communicating with either of them for the past eleven years. She doesn't attend any events where she may see them or could possibly run into them. Since 2005, Kyle hasn't been seen at any family event, including parties, graduations, or funerals, out of fear that she may be in the same vicinity as her mother or sister. It has gotten that deep.

Once upon a time, Irene and Kyle seemed close. Their dynamic changed after Kyle gave birth to her son. Irene's other grandchildren were born soon after Kyle's son was born and tensions grew within her family unit. Irene wanted her children and grandchildren to be close with one another and present a vastly different family than what she considered hers to be. Irene wanted her mother to see how good of a grandmother and matriarch she could be. The only problem was that, just as the generation before, Irene's children hadn't tempered their resentments toward each other and Irene when their own children were born. Dealing with parenthood and adulthood, they only became more aggressive toward one another.

Kyle bought her first house, shortly after I first moved to St. Louis, because she wanted her son to grow up in a house, and not in an apartment as she had. She remarked that buying a house was something that her mother had never done and she desired to provide her child with a better upbringing than what she had. Statements like that only increased tension between the two. Irene felt she had done her best as a single mother with four children, and Kyle clearly wanted her childhood to go much differently than it had.

After Kyle bought her first house, Irene and I moved in. The tensions between the two of them escalated quickly and to new heights. One day, Kyle assaulted Irene and abruptly put her out on the street. I moved out about a month after that and moved into my first apartment, a studio right next door to Irene. My goal was not to take sides, but to let Kyle have what she wanted. She was angry with her mother and let me know that she didn't want to take care of a grown man. Kyle and I didn't communicate as much afterwards, but she stopped talking to Irene altogether for over 4 years.

In 2005, Kyle's son, Irene's grandson, accused Irene and Mya of child abuse. As if Irene and Kyle's relationship hadn't had enough problems before, the allegation was a death blow to any hopes of reconciliation. They had only resumed contact just weeks leading up to the child abuse incident. Kyle felt bad that her son was growing up without a relationship with his grandmother or aunt because of the animosity between them. So she agreed to let them babysit him, since she needed a babysitter for him anyway.

The only people who really know what happened that day are Irene, Mya, and Kyle's son. I had just gotten off work and stopped by Irene's house as I usually did. Upon my arrival, I encountered an angry and flustered Kyle. When she saw me park, she hopped out of her vehicle and stopped me before I entered Irene's house. "Look what they did to him!" she yelled at me. I had no idea what she was talking about. "Look what they did to his face!" she continued to shout. I still had no idea what was going on. It never even crossed my mind who the "him" and "they" were. All I could say to her was, "Who?" She responded with some names for her mother and sister that I wouldn't have come up with in all my years of using foul language.

I went to her vehicle and peered in at her son on the passenger side. He was only about seven or eight years old at the time. He was bigger than most kids for his age but he was still very much a young child. One side of his face was bruised from his chin to his forehead. He was a fair-skinned boy, so the contrast was alarming. I could do no more than stand there with my mouth open. "Who did this to him?" I asked, still oblivious that Kyle was suggesting Irene and Mya had done this to her son. Her answer to my question didn't mention them by name, but only identified them by expletives.

I didn't know what to do, say, think, or even feel at the time. Kyle had called the police and was waiting on their arrival. She felt that she had allowed this to happen as his mother. Kyle believed that her son was attacked by her mother and sister as retribution for her assault on Irene a few years back. I wanted no parts of this one. I wished Kyle well and hopped in my car. I told her to call me if she needed me. There was no reason for me to involve myself in an incident as toxic as this one. These women were mothers and daughters and sisters and I was just a cousin and nephew. I felt bad for everyone involved but there was nothing I could do for any of them.

Irene and Mya presented themselves as victims. Irene said the allegations caused her to lose her nursing license and Mya to lose her teaching license. They had no choice but to move back to Bordentown. Kyle denies that she pressed charges on either of them and believes they left town out of fear that she would press charges.

Irene cut all ties with me because she felt that I was disloyal for not siding with her. She said that by me leaving, I put her in jeopardy of being imprisoned. I was supposed to defend her against the allegations made by Kyle. Irene's defense to the police was that her grandson had self-injured himself as part of a temper tantrum. She wanted me to attest that I had seen him act out in that manner before, which I honestly had not. I guess I was supposed to lie for her, against her own grandson, and since I didn't, I was disposable.

Ever since that day, things were never the same between Irene and I. I tried to discuss it with her years later at Camille's graduation but she was completely unreceptive. I remember apologizing to her for not being there in her time of need but I also explained that I was only doing what I thought was best for all of us. Although we hadn't completely reconciled, I thought she would get past it someday, as people usually do, but I gave her too much credit. After all, she was a member of my family, and letting go wasn't something that we did very well.

Living with Aunt Diane, Irene began going to church and went to school for theology. To think that after immersing oneself in faith, she could still be as unforgiving made me question her presentation of faith. Everything that my family seemed to do was questionable anymore. It was like I couldn't turn off the universe from revealing, and I also couldn't turn off my constant questioning of everything.

Kyle wasn't my favorite person either, at the time, but she was family and there was nothing wrong with keeping in touch. We stayed in contact and eventually started to talk on a regular basis. We cleared the air many years back and I consider us to be close now. There are no hard feelings on my part. Other than myself, she only kept in touch with Angela. Irene became close with my father when she moved back to Jersey, which created tension between him and Angela. With Irene there, he had someone else to depend on, which meant he didn't have to be as nice to Angela, if he didn't want to. I also think that Irene felt some kind of way about me from listening to my father and his side of what took place in our relationship.

My father told me that he had confided in Irene about the trouble that he and I had, to which she paralleled to her trouble with Kyle. He also made it clear to me that he did not believe that our relationship paralleled Irene and Kyle's. I agreed with him. Kyle vowed to never speak to her mother again or even be in her presence. My father and I had issues that we were working on but there was no hatred between the two of us. Still, I think that Irene wanted to lump Kyle and I together, so that she could make it seem like it wasn't just her that had a troubled relationship with a child.

It was the only explanation that I could come up with to explain Irene's passive aggressive attitude towards me when I arrived in Bordentown to see my father. Irene wasn't the only one who seemed strange, she was just more adept at exhibiting micro-aggressions than the others. From the moment that I stepped foot in the door, there was an elephant in the room. I could tell that some kind of discussion preceded my arrival. At any moment, I knew that I would be confronted by someone. No one in this family had ever been good with dealing with the elephant in the room. It's like they can't wait to address an issue or bring tension to the forefront.

The topic of the day seemed to be how long I planned on staying in New Jersey. Everyone asked me how long I was staying as if it was a burning question on everyone's mind. Inquiring minds wanted to know my plans for dealing with my father's passing. I told them I was going to leave in a few days and come back when I needed to, if I needed to. I hoped that if I put it out there that everything was going to be fine, just maybe a miracle would happen. Things were obviously pretty bad but it couldn't hurt to remain positive.

I also wanted to see their reactions to gauge what was going on behind my back. I packed enough clothes to last me a week, but I was going to check their temperatures first, before committing to staying for an entire week like I did the last time. They were always discussing one another behind each other's back and all of them had underlying issues with each other. I would've been a complete fool to believe that I was somehow exempt. In fact, the only time they would actually seem to unite was when there was a common target for them to attack. Of course, they would wait for Travis and I to go back to our hotel before they talked about us. They weren't honest enough to say anything to your face, or decent enough to give someone the opportunity to defend themselves.

There was always a target, otherwise they had nothing else to talk about. Since I was present, their target was their cousin Tootsy. Tootsy called to let Irene know that she was going to stop by, which prompted them to go on and on about how greedy Tootsy and her husband were.

When Aunt Diane died, she left her home and all of her belongings to her sister Aunt Valerie. Aunt Valerie's daughter, Tootsy, their cousin, was placed in charge of Aunt Diane's estate because Aunt Valerie suffers from

Alzheimer's Disease. My father, Etta, and Angela felt that Irene should've been given the house since she was Aunt Diane's caretaker at death. The only problem was that Aunt Diane didn't put that in her will nor did it align with what was set forth legally. Tootsy planned on selling the house, much to their chagrin. She ended up not selling the house because the money would've went to the state, since Aunt Valerie was being treated in a state hospital.

Since Tootsy didn't give them their way, they were compelled to defame her and rip her to pieces. Irene still got to live in the house but that wasn't good enough for anybody though. Why was I so concerned about what they were saying about Tootsy, someone who wasn't very close to me? It was none of my business but as I sat there and listened to them attack her character, I became increasingly annoyed. The things that they were saying about her were not only defaming but were completely unfounded. Irene even went as far as to say that Tootsy was jealous of her own mother because of how youthful Aunt Valerie looked. I don't know what that had to do with anything but it struck me as a low blow, especially for someone of such faith as she presented herself to be.

When Tootsy showed up to visit my father, she didn't knock on the door but instead used the key that she had. After all, she was the owner of the house. I can definitely understand how violated one must feel to know that someone would just enter your home, even if they own it, without asking for permission. Then I thought, if she's as bad as you all just made her out to be, why are you so surprised? Angela and Etta rushed to the bedroom to talk about the audacity that Tootsy had to just walk into the house. After listening to the way they had just talked about her, I thought she was well within her rights. Why did they think that they were the only people allowed to be mean or encroach upon others? Served them right, I thought.

While Angela and Etta went on and on in the other

room about how wrong Tootsy was, I went to the living room to see for myself. Tootsy had never presented herself to be anything but nice to me. I had just seen her at Aunt Diane's funeral and she was nice to me then. She and her husband told me how much they loved my spirit, so maybe I was a bit impartial. They were also very supportive of my relationship with Travis, which was refreshing, considering they were both members of the clergy. Perhaps, I was biased in my opinion of her, but I think that accusing her of being jealous of her own mother was completely uncalled for, even if it was true. I didn't believe it was true for a minute but even if it was, some opinions you keep to yourself. At least I did.

I sat and spoke with Tootsy for just a minute and she seemed pleasant as always. Irene was also extremely pleasant with her. She smiled from ear to ear and only spoke in the softest, sweetest, tone. Just moments before, she had accused her of being jealous of her own mother's youth and beauty. Irene also said that Tootsy didn't bother to get proper care for her ailing mother with Alzheimer's.

I've never been one of those people to hold Christians accountable for every little mistake they make, but I have met many people of faith and they operated much differently than Irene was. They made you feel good, talked people up, instead of putting people down. I was really bothered by it all, just as I was when Angela laid all of Mya's secrets out for anyone to salivate over. Irene, Angela, and Etta had just gone on and on about Tootsy's husband's visit to the bank to empty out Aunt Diane's account. Yet, Irene was smiling from ear to ear in Tootsy's face, just mere minutes after being so disgusted that Tootsy and her husband had bought a new Mercedes-Benz with money from Aunt Diane's insurance policy. It had to be the quickest change of heart in history or Irene was a major phony.

Before I left them alone to their conversation, I

asked Tootsy where the monument for my great-grandfather was located in town. Aunt Diane had told me about a monument built for the teachers of the No. 2 school, the first school for black children that was built in the town and my great-grandfather's name was on it. He and I shared the same name, so I thought it would be a cool sight to see. I was always intrigued by the fact that I became a teacher, just as he had, without even knowing our family had a legacy in education. Since I had recently left my teaching career behind, I felt, for some reason, that it would provide with me some sense of direction. That inner voice told me that if I went there, the universe would provide with me some guidance.

Tootsy lit up! She seemed surprised and proud that I was taking interest in the family legacy. There had always been a disconnect with the family in Bordentown, which was only furthered by incidents such as the handling of Aunt Diane's will.

Tootsy's directions were detailed and clear but only to someone who knew the local streets. We both laughed when I nodded and then asked for an address, so that I could "google" it. "I'm going to get lost trying to remember all those directions," I said. Tootsy laughed again. "You'll be lost regardless," said Irene dryly. Her delivery hit me in the pit of my stomach. Her entire tone changed when she said it and there was something very malicious in her tone. I know Irene very well, and she was trying to send a message, I just didn't know what it was.

Did she mean that there was no monument and that I would be looking for something that didn't exist? Etta, Angela, and Irene said that no such monument really existed. When they talked about it before, their tone struck me as odd. My thinking was that a monument with our family name on it would be something that everyone would be proud of. It must have been more important to maintain their division from the Bordentown members of the family who were so extremely proud of our legacy.

My gut told me that Irene was referring to something else, something pertaining to the way that she felt about me. She was trying to throw shade. If what I was feeling was in fact true, then that meant I was dealing with some real cruelty. All I could do was squint my eyes and purse my lips to keep from disrespecting her. Her words caused my stomach to burn, which meant that there was some potent negativity behind them. I removed myself and decided to leave immediately, in search of the monument with my great-grandfather's and my name on it.

Travis and I left to find the monument and to spend some time alone. All the negativity that was exuding from the family was overwhelming. It wouldn't have gotten to me, if I was still in the same negative space that they were in, but I wasn't. I had not only purged my negativity, but Travis had removed all of those protective emotional walls that I had built over 31 years. I was vulnerable and exposed around these people for the first time ever. I had never been around them without walls and defenses up, even as a kid. I wasn't prepared!

I could tell that everyone was containing feelings about me, and they were beginning to express them in their subtle ways, such as Irene's "lost" comments. Years ago, Irene would've been my biggest supporter throughout this entire ordeal but all of that had disintegrated over the years. She must have disregarded all of those heart-to-heart talks we had when I got on her bad side. She must have forgotten that she confided in me how much she despised her mother and Angela, or maybe she just saw an opportunity to do to me what she felt I had done to her years before. Love wouldn't do that though. Love is not vengeful.

All of the understanding that Irene had for me was gone because I hadn't acted in the manner that best suited her when she needed it. It didn't matter that she knew my heart, or that I revealed my true self to her, my true good.

Furthermore, it had been years and she still hadn't gotten past it. This was how everyone in the family operated. They never got past anything. The family was cursed and everyone inherited it, and passed it on to their children. A smile didn't mean anything, nor did a polite conversation. Once they disposed of someone, their "family" was nothing more than a facade. Where there is a facade, that means that something is being hidden. It was only a matter of time before this facade would fall and all that was hidden would be exposed.

CHAPTER NINE: APRIL 11, 2016

If a person doesn't feel loved, are they to blame for their feelings or are their feelings indicative of something that is actually happening? Are the things that we feel created by truth, intuition, or just prior experiences? I believe that our feelings are divine protection from a multitude of external forces. When we feel things, we are receiving cues from the universe and a higher power. GOD provides us with feelings for our own protection and advancement. Feelings signal us to change our thoughts or the direction that we may be moving in. When we are in disharmony with the universe, we feel bad. When we are in harmony, we feel wonderful, abundant, and happy. Things that make us feel good, we pursue. Things that make us feel bad, we avoid. No matter what people do or say, we never forget the way they make us feel. But what happens when no matter what a person does to prove themselves to you, you still have bad feelings?

For as long as I searched for love, never had it crossed my mind that *I* may not know how to love. It was becoming clear that no one in my family really knew how to love. Our love was conditional and easily revoked whenever the person we loved no longer abided by our conditions. There was also an automated tendency to tear apart and destroy the very people who you supposedly love.

Out of my father and his sisters, only Angela had managed to maintain her marriage, and whose to say that wasn't a facade also. Everything pertaining to the family was questionable to me at this point. The rest of them all ended up alone after nasty breakups. The common denominator was them. I didn't want to love like them, especially not after falling in love with Travis.

I couldn't put my finger on exactly what was going

to happen or why it was going to happen, but I just had this feeling that the end of a lot more than just my father's life was upon me. The universe kept impressing upon me that I would soon be cutting ties with everyone. I just didn't know what was going to be the final straw. I couldn't stand their negative energy, but I knew it wasn't enough to warrant burning a bridge. Yet, I knew that the burning of bridges was on the horizon.

As my father continued to slip away, what remained of the facade of the family died quickly and without protest. The tone and tension in the room evolved into bold action and blatant disrespect. What started as an elephant in the room, grew into a full blown circus.

Things started to escalate when I took a phone call from a casting agency. I had scheduled to meet with a casting agency in Phoenix before all of this had taken place. The appointment was in a day or two, and they were calling to confirm. Etta and Angela listened and interjected, advising me to cancel and stay longer.

I still hadn't decided how long I was going to stay, but Travis had to leave out the next morning. I also hadn't decided whether I was going to leave with him or stay. Deep down inside, I couldn't wait to leave, but I still felt being there was my obligation. I didn't want to be apart from Travis, and I didn't want to be around family at all, but I did want to stay for my father.

For the rest of the day, Etta walked around with a sour ass look on her face. She was trying to show me she disagreed with me. Little did she know, I hadn't made my mind all the way up but her sour ass face was making it up for me. By the end of our last night, the house was filled with so much negativity that I knew I had to leave.

People continued to come in and out as the day turned into night. Mya showed up and immediately began troublemaking. First, she pried and questioned Travis about any and everything she could think of. Then, she felt the need to share *all* of her personal problems. As my father clung to life in the other room, Mya complained about the acne on her face and the few pounds that she had gained.

Even with her extra pounds, she was still a toothpick. Travis advised her to work on whatever was going on within to change what showed up on the outside. Mya went on and on about how stressed out she had been recently, but wasn't clear about what the cause of her stress was. Maybe my father's illness was wearing on her, or maybe it was the affair she was having that was causing her so much stress.

Of course a conversation with Mya couldn't just be pleasant or without controversy. She just had to slip in a dig about Travis' weight after he was nice enough to listen to her complain about her trivial and petty problems. Apparently, she thought that everyone dreamed of being super skinny, just because her weight was something that she was insecure about and obsessed over.

Travis is a handsome man, perfectly proportioned, and built just right for me. He stands at 6-feet, 3-inches tall and could very well play professional football, just like the married man that Mya was sleeping with. Travis wasn't fat or flabby, by any means. He complimented my 6-feet, 4-inch height and basketball player build perfectly.

Mya continued to try Travis since she wasn't able to get a reaction out of him the first time. The nerve of her, I thought. I had googled the football player that she was having an affair with. Not only was he more than big, according to the standards she was applying to Travis, he was hard on the eyes, or at least my eyes. And he was married, but I guess that was supposed to be a secret.

It's funny how people will run off at the mouth when they think you don't know of all the dirt that they try to hide. Not only did I have that dirt on her, Kyle had told me so much dirt on both Irene and Mya, they would have a reason to hate me for real, if I ran off at my mouth.

Mya always found a way to insult or judge people. It was like she lacked basic social skills. That was why I never bothered to deal with her. It never failed for her to say something rude or insulting for no apparent reason. I remember when a friend of mine and I tried to hang out with her some years back, and she made disparaging comments about the fact that we smoked cigarettes. She went on and on about how nasty we were, comparing smoking to licking a toilet seat. Nobody cares that she had an opinion about anything, but you don't have to share it with people. I had plenty of opinions about the things that she did, but it was not my place to always impose them on her.

Travis seemed to handle himself well amidst all of her comments. I was ready to slap her, so I excused myself from the kitchen. I went into Aunt Diane's bedroom with Shay as a way to try and keep the peace. Shay was always a breath of fresh air when dealing with the family. She is a shallow and unaware young woman, which means she usually has no idea of the drama or what is going on in the family. All she cared about was hair, makeup, and guys. She was like an escape from reality.

I viewed Shay like a little sister since the day she was born. For many years, I was her babysitter when I spent nights at Angela's house. Angela made sure that if I stayed at her house, that I earned my keep and watching her daughter was just one of the many ways that I earned my keep. Looking back on it, taking care of Shay groomed me to work with children as an adult. When I became a teacher, I had already been used to taking care of children. It's an example of how all of our experiences contribute to our whole experience in some way.

Shay and I blew off about thirty minutes going live on Facebook, giving out hair and makeup advice. Well, Shay gave out hair and makeup advice. I just ran my mouth. Etta came in the room with us and continued to stare at me the with the same sour ass face. I continued to ignore her. She chain-smoked a few cigarettes and then stormed back out of the bedroom. When she stormed out, something told me to go and check on Travis.

When I went back into the kitchen, Etta was nose to nose with Travis. She had just finished saying something but her volume was so low that it was inaudible. When she saw me, she immediately scattered. Travis was visibly upset and outdone by whatever she had said to him.

When I asked him what was said, he said he didn't want to talk about. His face said enough though. I probed him more and then he told me that she was pressuring him to get me to stay in town longer.

"You want to know my opinion?" interjected Mya. "No, I don't," I replied without hesitation. Mya completely ignored me and went on to share her unsolicited and unwanted opinion with Travis. "We appreciate you coming, but we really need him to stay here," she continued.

I had just told Mya we didn't care to hear her opinion! Before she could get out another sentence, I cut her completely off, something everyone in the family was good at. "Didn't I just tell you I didn't want your opinion." I adjusted my tone and demeanor to let her know that I wasn't about to go back and forth with her. She needed to shut up as far as I was concerned. If she would've said one more thing, she would've gotten embarrassed in that kitchen. I owed her one anyway. More than one, actually. She had tried me too many times over the years.

After that, there was no way that we could've stayed another night in New Jersey. I felt bad about leaving my father in such condition, but I hated these bitches and I wasn't going to be able to stay without losing my cool. I just couldn't do it.

Etta, drunk and belligerent made herself the mouthpiece for the entire family. She came back into the kitchen and exploded, screaming and yelling, and threatening me. She made it evident that I had been the topic of discussion before I got there, confirming my intuition. "If you leave, you're going to regret it for the rest of your life," she threatened.

I remained calm, almost like a statesman at a debate. I didn't want to be like them in any way, shape, or form. My father was just on the other side of the wall and I didn't want to make the situation worse. They were a disgusting group of people who had no regard for sanctity or civility. No one could understand or even attempted to understand my feelings, so it was off with my head.

After yelling, screaming, and acting like a drunken fool, Etta was all out of shenanigans, so she told me to leave. She wasn't able to bully me into doing what she wanted so it was time for me to go. I was being put out again. History was repeating itself. The only problem for Etta was that this was not her house and she couldn't put me out.

Angela heard us and came in the kitchen to intervene. The first thing she said was, "He (my father) can hear you in the other room!" Etta responded by telling Angela to mind her business, which only made Angela become combative as well. It was one of Angela's trigger points because everyone was always talking about how she gossiped and involved herself in people's business. "You promised you wouldn't argue!" Angela pleaded. "I'm going to say something, if ain't nobody else going to say something!" Etta boasted. It was more confirmation that they had all been discussing me behind my back.

Then, the arguing between Etta and Angela soon transformed into the recurring argument they had been having for 40 years. It was how the arguments always went. Something in the moment created tension and led to a disagreement. Then the disagreement about one thing turned into a fight about everything that they had ever said or done to one another in their whole life. Screaming led to pursing of lips and damn near growling. Angela and her husband abruptly left and Etta retreated to Aunt Diane's room. "I gotta go before I kick her f--king ass!" was Angela's exit statement.

I began to feel sick. My head was hot and my stomach was also on fire. The entire ordeal was pathetic to me. What kind of people would behave in this manner, with a dying man in the very next room? I'm sure many would but not anyone that I wanted to surround myself with.

Travis and I sat in the kitchen and stared at one another. I hadn't felt this terrible in years. Then, I pinpointed the last time I had felt like this. It was when I was a teenager and they were the cause of it then.

So many years had passed and they were still the only people that could make me feel this bad. No one else in my life had ever caused me so much grief. I was infuriated that I had allowed this to happen again. Everything that I had forgiven them for was happening again before my eyes. Nothing had changed, except my perspective.

As angry as I was, I had to accept the fact that I created this monster. It wasn't intentional, but I still had to take accountability for what I had done. Years prior, when I thought I had done the work I needed to do to better myself, I only did a half-ass job. Instead of addressing all that had ever happened to me, I just placed the blame on my parents for not preventing it from happening to me. I rejected my mother and father out of resentment and let everyone else in the family off the hook.

For years, I convinced myself that if my parents had been better parents then I wouldn't have had to go through all that I went through at the hands of others. I had easily forgiven Angela, Irene, and Etta but I struggled to forgive my mother and father, holding them to a higher level of accountability. It was clear to me now though, the things that I went through were a collective effort, and I needed to hold everyone accountable. I shouldn't have been treated the way that I was treated and I shouldn't have been treated the way I was being treated.

Mya was having a field day as the family imploded. She actually smiled and saw nothing disheartening about the situation. She was content to have so much drama going on. Seconds after Angela left, Mya made sure to have Etta rehash the entire incident from just the other room. As my heart broke in the kitchen, I could hear Mya and Etta attacking my character, and laughing about what happened.

Aunt Diane's house was small, so the intention was for me to hear everything that was said. That moment, I understood why Kyle refused to have any contact with Mya. Mya was toxic and had no regard for the fact that people's feelings were hurt or the severity of the situation. Instead, her focus was on stirring the pot and turning the knife deeper in everyone's wounds.

Etta and Angela were completely out of control and didn't know how to control their emotions or express them appropriately. Their emotional role model was my grandmother, who only knew how to express her emotions by screaming, hollering, and using profanity.

I was disgusted to think that *I* had ever carried on in such a manner, but I had many times before. At one point in my life, I was just as miserable as Mya and would've been just as excited to see a good fight. It's why people in poverty love to fight and instigate fights. When you are stuck in a negative space, you gravitate towards negativity because it's all that you know or are used to. I can only thank GOD for how far I've came.

I thought that Irene would've tried to buffer her daughter's behavior, but she made no attempt. She let Mya continue to heckle and Etta to gloat about fighting from the next room for all of us to hear. For a moment, it seemed as if Irene attempted to understand me but she was actually only trying to make the moment about herself.

I attempted to explain why I felt the need to leave to Irene and she paralleled it to her feelings toward her mother. Not only did she find a way to make it about her, but I was uncomfortable with the parallel because I didn't have any volatility toward my father as she had toward her mother. We weren't leaving because I had animosity toward my father or didn't care. We were leaving because I felt like shit being in the company of my father's family, Irene included. After that night, I no longer identified them as my family, they were his family from that point on. I will not own their energy nor accept it.

Travis and I made our way to the door, knowing that we would probably never see my father alive again. We went to his bedside to say goodbye. He talked to Travis first, and told him to take care of me. I told my father that I would see him in a couple days, sticking with the mindset that I would remain positive and uplifting. We planned to come back on Travis' next off days.

My father struggled to breath and his talking had become incoherent, but in that moment he sat up in his bed and spoke in a crystal clear voice. "Keep that spirit up!" he said. Those were the last words he said to me and I'm content with them.

I wondered if he heard his sister go at it with me or was he just speaking in general about my spirit. Being around his family, it's easy to get your spirit down. I promised him that I wouldn't get my spirit down and I've worked very hard since then to keep it up. At that time, I thought I had seen everyone at their lowest. What was still to come would show me that I hadn't touched the tip of the iceberg that night.

My fingers typed like crazy on the plane ride back to Phoenix. I wasn't working on *From Scratch* though. I didn't know what I was working on, I just started typing without direction about everything that had taken place. My thoughts couldn't keep up with my fingers. For the entire five-hour flight, my head was down, focused on what I was writing.

Years of working on myself and all of my growth hadn't prepared me to feel like a helpless child once again. If I could feel the way that I felt when I was a kid around my family as 32-year old man, that meant that I hadn't fully dealt with my issues. The whipping boy that was there as a kid hadn't went away or grown into a man, he had just hidden himself from me. They still saw him.

I was happier than ever before to be in Phoenix after spending two days with my father's family, even happier than when I returned after the first trip. Just a day gone from their presence was enough to make me feel better. I was so grateful for what Phoenix had to offer, that my negative thoughts surrounding my father and his family were offset.

It didn't last very long. My father passed early in the morning on April 11, 2016, just two days after we returned to Phoenix. The next day, Etta, Irene, Angela, and Camille made funeral arrangements at a funeral home in Woodbury. Although he had no insurance policy or money in the bank, they spared no expense. The funeral arrangements came to a grand total close to $13,000.

That same day, I was notified that I had to come up with the money for my father's funeral arrangements by that Thursday. Everything was happening so quickly that I could barely come to terms with reality. Not only was the amount for the funeral way more than I had imagined, I had no idea how I was going to pay for it.

I spoke with the funeral home about financing and was quickly rebuffed. If I didn't have the money by Thursday, they were not going to proceed with burying my father. They had scheduled his funeral for that Saturday, April 16, so I had to act quickly. I couldn't fathom why they would arrange the funeral to be just 5 days later and why it was so expensive. If I was going to have to pay for it all on my own, why didn't they wait for me to make arrangements.

The more that I thought about it, I felt like a game was being played after a while. I was put under pressure to come up with $13,000 in 4 days without any help. No one offered any help toward the final expenses or any of our travel expenses. No one seemed concerned about the cost or how I was going to come up with the money. For the first time in history, everyone in his family was minding their own business.

This must have been my consequence for going against the family and leaving that night in Bordentown. I had studied them long enough and I knew what they were up to. They wanted to teach me a lesson for not doing as they said. It was the way that they operated.

Etta said that I would regret leaving for the rest of my life. I guess this was the beginning. These people of his, my father's family, were trying to prove something to me or trying to break me. How completely inappropriate was it to use such a devastating time to play games? My father was dead and they saw it as an opportunity to flex on me.

This $13,000 was going to completely wipe out my savings and force me back into a position in life that I was working so hard to get away from. I was not working at the time because I had left my job to move to Arizona.

I contemplated not answering the phone and disappearing. My father had not helped me financially with anything as an adult and he was not the father that I wanted him to be as a child. He was verbally abusive and unsupportive. I thought about the times that he called me a faggot and the time that he slapped me right across the side of my face. The things he said about my mother ran through my mind. And now, in death, he was going to financially set me back.

All of the things that I went through, he played a

pivotal role in. My father had been more of a detriment than an asset to my life. But, I had forgiven him for all of it and I was in a better place because I forgave him. I had moved past all of it and chose to live the way GOD tells us to. I was blessed because I followed GOD's instructions to forgive. I had an amazing life and all of those negative experiences were in my past. So, why was I thinking of all of these negative feelings that I had gotten past? Was I really past it all?

CHAPTER TEN: IN REMEMBERANCE OF ME

If necessity is the mother of invention, then it's also related to change somehow. Learning how to be still had been my goal for quite some time, and I had made much progress toward that goal. After being presented with a $13,000 funeral bill for my father, all my working at being still became obsolete. I realized very quickly that stillness didn't require any effort. Saddled with the largest bill I've ever had in my life, I didn't have a clue what to do, and for the first time in my life, I accepted that there was nothing that I could do.

So, I did nothing. I was still. I didn't call anyone and I didn't talk about it with Travis. Whatever was going to happen was going to happen. The entire scenario was beyond my control and comprehension. In my stillness, GOD revealed to me that the devil, the enemy, was trying to take me back to where I had been. The enemy was using death and the emotions that came with it to destroy all of my progress.

More specifically, it was the actions of his family that had put me back in such a negative place. The devil had used them and they didn't even know it. In fact, the devil had used them for many years and they didn't even know it.

I had a choice to make and had to make it quickly. I could give in to fear, afraid that I would lack after spending my savings on a funeral. I could reignite my old resentments and anger toward my father or I could act upon my faith and out of love. I chose to walk in faith and allow whatever was going to happen to happen.

Travis suggested that we each pay $5000 and put the rest on a credit card. That way, I wouldn't completely deplete my savings. His goal was for me not to stress about the situation and focus on putting my father to rest properly. I couldn't help but feel better knowing that Travis was supporting me. I may have not had any support from a so-called "family," but I had my future husband who would do anything to see me happy and succeed. Having his support strengthened our bond and made me love him even more than I already did. It was a positive takeaway from a situation that the devil had intended to be so negative.

Travis and I made airline arrangements, hotel accommodations, and headed out. I knew that I could get through as long as I had him by my side. We rented a black Cadillac in my father's honor. He loved Cadillacs and since we were going to pay so much money, we figured that we might as well do it all with style and class. My father would have been proud of how we handled our business and the manner in which we handled it.

When we got to New Jersey, I had absolutely no desire to speak to or bother with a single family member. They had all left me out to dry. Something kept nudging me to believe that they had ran up a $13,000 bill on purpose and that they were doing nothing to help on purpose. I tried to dismiss my feelings but to no avail. Whenever my mind tried to dismiss what my heart was telling me, my mind ended up agreeing with heart. My mind and my heart were on the same page. How often does that happen?

No matter how hard I tried, I couldn't convince myself that they were not up to no good. The fact that everyone was so hands off after making the arrangements struck me as odd. These were the same people who had so many opinions about our relationship and how things between us played out.

Just days before, Etta wanted to put me out because I was planning on leaving town in the morning. Suddenly, everyone was just keeping to themselves. I had seen many families prepare for a funeral service but never in the way my family was preparing for this one. Many people die without life insurance, and usually a family raises funds together to make sure that person receives a proper burial. This wasn't the case for me though. I was completely on my own.

Kyle called me to let me know that she would not be making it to the funeral. Her reasoning was what it had always been. She knew that Mya and Irene would be there and she refused to be around them.

I told Kyle my feelings and suspicions about what the family was up to. Kyle wouldn't provide the details about what she knew, but she said their goal was to force me into a corner so I would have to ask them for help. Angela had called Kyle to pressure her into showing up at the funeral, and spilled the beans about what their plan was. Angela can never keep her mouth shut.

Kyle said she would fill me in with all the details when everything was over. She said it was too much to add to the already stressful situation I was under. It was all that I needed to hear, I didn't need the details. If their plan was to run up a bill, so that I would be forced to ask them to help me pay, that plan failed. Who does that?

Asking represented more to them than just me needing them. Asking represented me being lower than them. It represented them having a level of power and control. The fact that I would have to ask them meant that my future husband wasn't in a position to help me. There were many layers to this little plan they hatched.

What bothered me the most, was that they would use my father's death to try and humiliate me. There was not one ounce of compassion for me or the loss of my father. This was their opportunity to knock me back down to that little boy who they had treated like crap. I wasn't that little boy though, and I didn't need a dime from them. Not only did I not need their money, I didn't need them.

Since I knew what their objective was, I wanted to show them just how unnecessary they were in my life. I focused on burying my father with dignity, and making them feel useless during the process.

The first step in ensuring he was buried with dignity was to rewrite his obituary. The funeral home sent a draft that oozed with the family's signature brand of sensationalism. At first, I didn't say anything about the obituary because it was obvious that someone had worked really hard to create an image of my father. Once I found about their little plan, I didn't give a damn anymore.

They could all be writers, if they wanted to be, I just choose to actually write. Nearly everyone of them has revised, omitted, and distorted facts to make themselves look innocent or better. The rewriting of my father's history had already began in the weeks preceding his death. I was reminded constantly of how proud my father was of me and how he talked about me all the time. That is why it was so important for me to be by his side during his sickness. They were foreshadowing about the direction that they were going to take after his passing.

As I read the draft of the obituary, I couldn't help but feel a sense of sorrow for my father. His real life should have been good enough and it didn't need to be sensationalized. And who was the sensationalism for? My father was dead and would reap no benefit from an overblown portrayal of his life. His obituary was written to make the family look good, the people he had left behind.

The obituary omitted much of who *he* was. There was a nickname that I had never heard anyone call him inserted in between his first and last name. There was a very sweet line about him being "Pop Pop" to his five grandchildren. It was very sweet and a complete lie at the same time. My father did treat my sister as his own and called her his daughter, but he had only just met her oldest son for the first time in January. He had never met her other four children. They were removed from her home and placed into foster care when they were young children. He was never affectionately called "Pop Pop" by anyone. My sister hadn't even been called "mom" in over a decade, so how was he "Pop Pop?"

I thought it was important that my sister and mother attend his funeral and I wanted them to be listed in his obituary, along with the five grandchildren, minus the sensationalism of the term "Pop Pop." I didn't want my father's life to be trivialized by lies and exaggerations. If he wanted to be affectionately called "Pop Pop," then he would have been that to someone. He lived his life the way that he chose and there is value in his truth, not a lie.

I took it upon myself to rewrite his obituary after no one seemed to know who wrote the original draft. Everyone said that the funeral director had used a template and that it was full of his exaggerations. I didn't believe that the funeral director's template included the term "Pop Pop," which is what we used to call my grandfather, but I went along with the story. Since no one took credit for it, I figured no one would be offended by a rewrite.

My goal was not to rewrite my father's history or make his life seem better than what it was. Instead, I wanted to paint him as a beautiful person by highlighting the beauty in his existence. He was a fervent problem-solver and lover of history. In those respects, he reminded me of myself.

I wrote about him as if I was an objective observer, or just a talented writer. I wanted to represent him in the way that he represented himself without inserting any of my own emotions or our experiences. I included the facts. He was married, had a son and a daughter, and five grandchildren. I didn't embellish or sensationalize any of it and I didn't need to. My rewrite touched my heart and painted my father in a positive light because he was amazing just the way he was. We all are.

The day before the funeral, we attended a private viewing at the funeral home. I don't know why it was necessary but we had already paid for it, so Travis and I made sure to show up. The private viewing was the first time that we were all together since his passing and the first time everyone was together since Etta and Angela nearly came to blows.

The funeral director waited for Travis and I to arrive before he allowed anyone to enter the funeral home. They were all standing in the parking lot waiting. No one had even bothered to get dressed properly. It was just another example of how nothing was making sense. What was the purpose of having this private viewing and not even bothering to get dressed?

Once we all packed into the sitting area, the director asked if we wanted to go back as a family, or if Travis and I wanted to go first. Travis made sure to interject before anyone else could. We were definitely going back first. It was my way of showing them that I was separating myself from them, once and for all.

In the viewing room, I remember Travis rubbing my back as I let out a single, warm tear. My father looked amazing in the casket which bothered me for some reason. They had even placed a smile on his face. I wanted more for him once I realized that he was gone forever. I wanted him to have experienced love like I had, traveled, and saw the world.

Once his family entered, there was an immediate shift in the energy. I didn't want to look at anyone, let alone talk to them. For the first couple of minutes, we just sat there and looked at the casket.

The funeral director brought in a DVD that he had created with pictures. The backdrop was a printing press, a testament to my father's years working for the newspaper. Seeing his life flash on the screen was quite emotional and I began to really feel like a piece of me was gone. The piece of me that he was definitely wasn't perfect, but he was still a piece of me.

The silence subsided after watching the video and everyone shed a tear. I tried to focus on Travis and no one else, in order to avoid showing my emotions. I wasn't trying to hide my sadness, I wanted to mask the contempt I had for them. I made an effort to be cordial in the small talk but I couldn't. For a moment, I started to feel that maybe I was being too hard on them.

GOD must have been paying attention to me at the very moment I had that thought. Within seconds, Irene reminded me of just how devious these people were.

We were all sitting in a reflective state when Irene hopped up and announced that she was leaving to go find an outfit. We had only been there about fifteen minutes. Her exact words were "Well bruh, I'd love to stick around but I gotta find me an outfit for tomorrow!" It was tacky and borderline disrespectful. Her announcement broke through all emotion and somberness in the room. It was like someone had rang the alarm for everyone to leave. Just like that, the private viewing was over.

It was their cue to exit, each one with a different reason. As Travis and I watched them leave, I wondered what the purpose of all this was. Why have a private viewing and leave after 15 minutes? It was as if they had all planned to leave once Irene made the announcement. The private viewing was their idea, it cost about $1500, and they only stayed for 15 minutes.

Getting my mother and sister to come was an additional expense on top of everything else. I sent my sister money through Western Union and she drove them up from Virginia. I told her I would give her enough money to get back once they arrived.

They showed up the morning of the funeral and in true form, they both made quite a splash. My sister showed up with a man I had never met or heard of before and my mother brought her cousin, just in case she had a run in with my father's sisters. Seeing my sister with yet another strange man was disheartening to say the least. Who would bring a date to a funeral? It wasn't like he knew my father or they were even dating seriously. Never mind the fact that she had to borrow money from me to make it to the funeral. I am a firm believer that a woman should not have to ask for anything if she has a man. If so, there is no reason for her to have the man with her.

I hadn't been to Bethel AME church since I was a child. We weren't the churchgoing family. My father had become more active in the church during the more recent, latter years of his life, and so had Irene, although I had doubts about her motives.

Bethel AME was exactly the way I remembered it. Exactly. It was clear that not many others were into the church because it hadn't been updated. The word *hymn* was still spelled out in block letters, on a wooden bulletin board, with no hymn listed underneath it. Two vases with fake white flowers still sat on each side of the pulpit. The only thing I didn't notice was "Do this in remembrance of me," engraved in the altar. It may still be there; I just don't remember seeing it. The phrase always caught my attention when I used to stare off into space when I was supposed to be listening to the preacher.

Bethel was our family church and we considered it to be our church home. However, we only frequented on Easter Sunday and the weeks preceding. As kids, we had to memorize our Easter pieces, so we went for the weeks leading up to Easter.

Easter pieces are bible verses that all the children would recite on Easter Sunday. Camille and I would always get Genesis 1:1..."In the beginning, GOD created the heavens and the Earth." The Sunday School teachers gave us Genesis 1:1 because that's the one that everybody knew and since we didn't go to church or Sunday School, they made it easy for us.

Every Easter, Camille and I would go to church

dressed in our very best, with some quarters or even a dollar to put in the collection plate. We knew you did not go to church without money for the collection plate. Most of the time, it was just Camille and I going to church, maybe Etta's daughter if she was in town. We would get dropped off and picked back up.

The adults never went to church, unless it was for a funeral or a wedding. They didn't seem interested in church one bit. Every now and then, they would talk about GOD but never with any depth or testimony. GOD was who they went to when they needed something. They were much more into drinking and having a good time.

Camille's parents, Angela and Carl, were always having get-togethers at their house or going to drink at one of their friend's houses. It seemed like everyone that was a friend of the family liked to drink just as much as them and many of them even had their own bars in the basements of their homes.

My father liked to go *out* to drink. He frequented bars in not so nice areas at least three to four nights a week. When he would work, he would go to bars and drink after his shift. I thought he went because he had a drinking problem. Now I know that it was a place where he was accepted, liked, and could be himself. He didn't have that at home or within his family.

Angela and my grandmother constantly told my father that he had a drinking problem even though the entire family drank heavily. They made him feel so bad that he eventually attended meetings to help him with alcoholism. The real problem he had was that he would lash out at his family when he would get drunk. All of the times that he let them diminish him or kept quiet would build up and when he drank, he would let out all of his frustration.

They said the same thing about Etta when she would lash out on them. Angela drank just as much, if not more, and lashed out just as much, if not more than both Etta and my father. But because she was Angela, her drinking wasn't considered a problem.

In spite of all the drinking, profanity, and dysfunction, his family wanted to appear as though they were god-fearing people in church. They work hard to always fit in wherever they are, church was no exception.

The day of the funeral was also no different. Irene was the leader of the pack since she had become holier than thou. This was the second time I watched her cut up in church since her spiritual rebirth; the first time was Aunt Diane's funeral.

Irene made sure to play up her faith in church, for attention if you ask me. Watching Irene in church was like watching a textbook reenactment of how to prove you're a believer in church. She said "Amen," every thirty to forty seconds and schooled her sisters on the church etiquette. All she needed was a giant hat and a worn down bible to complete the look.

Irene made sure to take her place in the front of the church as she was now the oldest surviving member of the family, the newly crowned matriarch of a dysfunctional bunch. She relished in all the attention that was bestowed upon her. It was as if she wanted to overshadow me that day. She was the first to jump up and speak for the family, not that I wanted to anyway.

The pastor read at least five letters of condolence from other churches that were specifically addressed to my father's sisters, nieces, nephews, and friends. There was no mention of me in any of them. It was an interesting omission, especially since Irene was mentioned by name in every one of them, and she was responsible for requesting the letters. Irene had given the churches all the information that was listed in the letters, and I was left out.

Bethel is a small church and it quickly filled up with locals, many who didn't even like my father but came to see him off. I know they didn't like him because he didn't like them. The small town mentality is strange like that. People showed up to say goodbye that more than likely never even said hello to him. The people in this town had nothing to do with my father while he was alive, yet everyone carried on like they loved him.

I resented the people in town almost just as much as I resented his family. Together, his family and the town had broken him down and tried to break me down. Ever since his accident as a teenager, the people in the town looked down on him. I knew how he felt because they looked down on me as well, but for being gay. With my father gone, and no more connections to his family, I didn't have to ever come back, unless it was on my own terms. When I buried my father, I was also going to bury all the lies, pain, and heartache that I suffered in this town.

Most of the service, I felt as if I was an illegitimate child at my father's funeral. There were people there that had no idea that he was married or that he had a son. Some of them were borderline rude but I told myself that I was just being emotional.

The pastor of the church was a former teacher of mine at the high school named Mr. Ruff. What were the odds of that one? It only made the situation seem more surreal. Mr. Ruff's daughters went to the same school and he and I had plenty of run-ins. Nevertheless, Mr. Ruff didn't hold any of my childish antics against me or my father. I was actually relieved to see that he would be honoring my father. He was someone that I knew had a relationship with both my father and I and would be respectful and genuine. That's another thing about small towns; you never know what capacity or circumstance that you may run into someone again.

Throughout the service, I learned things about my father that I had never known. Mr. Ruff spoke about his relationship with GOD and it resonated with me because I was working on my relationship with GOD. His best friend spoke of how they went to dip in the Atlantic Ocean every year on New Year's Day. I had no clue about that but I had just visited the ocean following his private viewing. The ocean has always been a place of refuge and reflection for me.

Mr. Ruff joked about how he was never afraid to tell his story, referencing my father's tendency to talk your ears off. I immediately thought about my story that I was working on, that I wanted to share with everyone.

Seeing my father laid out in a casket had to be the most surreal sight I had ever seen. I simply couldn't believe that this man, who played such a pivotal role in my life, good or bad, was going to be buried. Everything that had happened between us didn't matter anymore. My father was leaving me, alone on Earth, forever. This was the most major event I had ever experienced in my life.

The hardest part of the funeral was when I had to place a handkerchief over my father's face and close his casket. It was a tradition for the eldest son to perform for his father. Irene asked me if I wanted her to do it, another attempt for her to get attention. I declined her offer and committed to fulfilling my duties as a son. She didn't genuinely want to help; she was only trying to further diminish me.

Ultimately, I was proud of the service and the amount of people that came to see my father, whether I cared for them or not. The preparations and professionalism of the funeral home staff provided some consolation with regard to all the money that we had spent. Angela, Irene, and Etta put together a tip for Mr. Ruff and the choir. They didn't consult with me about tipping anyone, which was interesting since every other expense had been my sole responsibility. It was obvious that they were just trying to keep up appearances. They were willing to pay for something in public, without being asked, but in private they wouldn't contribute, unless they were asked.

As the pallbearers carried my father down the church stairs, I overheard my mother talking to my father's sisters. The pleasantries were completely false, awkward, and ill-timed. Angela invited her to stop by her house afterward.

Irene was tacky as hell, once again. She couldn't think of anything else to say to my mother other than that she only saw her at funerals. My mother had only seen Irene twice in her life. The first time was when my mother sang at my grandfather's funeral and the second time being my father's funeral.

The tone and exchanges were meant to make outsiders believe that this family was just like any other. The truth was that my father's sisters were horrible to my mother, didn't respect her, and couldn't wait to trash her as soon as she got from within earshot

Travis and I made our way to our black Cadillac rental. I was trying to dodge my mother, to keep her from riding with us. I didn't want to spend my time listening to her or having to tend to her needs. I only wanted to worry about my own emotions. We had parked directly behind the hearse, anticipating that we would follow directly behind my father's body. The funeral director had reserved the spot for us and gave us a brief tutorial before the service started.

The funeral director's skill set impressed me. I wondered: Did he really enjoy his job or did he ever want to do something else? Maybe he really just wanted to be an event planner, or even a wedding planner but ended up planning funerals. When we first met him, he told us that he could perform weddings after Travis and I told him we were engaged. He would be good at planning anything, if he could deal with death all the time.

When it was time to go to the cemetery, the funeral director approached the driver's side of our black Cadillac and informed Travis of the route we would be taking to the burial site. He also informed us that Tootsy's husband was going to follow behind the hearse because he's a minister. Travis and I would follow directly after Tootsy's husband. As we waited to pull off, cars begin to pull up beside us. Irene hopped in the car with Tootsy's husband and without hesitation waved three cars to hop right in front of us in the procession. Irene had been to enough funerals in her day, so she had to know that there was an order to the procession. Travis tried to pull off to enter the procession and we almost had an accident. It was obvious, no one had any regard for me. We ended up being the 8th car in the procession, diminished yet again.

CHAPTER ELEVEN: EATING SINS

When I lived in St. Louis, I had a friend named Rosie many years back. When her father died, I remember cooking for the family as my way of contributing to them during their loss. The repast was held at her mother's house and it was a very intimate affair.

Her mother would not eat any of the food that I had prepared. When I asked her about it, she said she didn't eat at funerals. She said that when you ate at a man's funeral, you ate his sins. I never forgot that little tidbit and I took it with me whenever I attended a funeral afterward. It never made sense to me to feed people after a funeral anyway, like it was some kind of party.

My father's repast was closer to a party than any repast I had ever been to. Angela and Etta reserved a banquet hall with catering and full service. Their reason for having a catered space was so that they wouldn't have to cook. I couldn't help but think about how I had cooked for Rosie's family, but my family was too good for that these days. I had actually considered skipping the entire thing but Travis reminded me that it was about respecting my father and not about anyone else there. Remembering that I had pledged to do this thing with dignity, I showed up...late.

We stopped at a liquor store prior to going to the repast. I knew that I would need to be intoxicated to keep a positive attitude for the rest of the day. Apparently, our trip to the liquor store delayed the service of the food. When we arrived, the manager was visibly irritated. They were waiting for me to arrive to serve the food. It would've been too obvious to disregard me this time. As soon as I got there, the go ahead was given and those people swarmed the buffet line.

My mother decided not to stay for the repast. Instead, she went to spend time with her family. She probably didn't appreciate how distant I was with her. She just didn't know how hard it was for me that day. From the moment I woke up, I felt like I was dying myself. I didn't care about anyone in the world; I was doing all that I could to survive.

The fact that I had started drinking as soon as we left the cemetery didn't help my mood either. It only sent me into "I don't give a f--k" autopilot. I had already started drinking en route from the burial to the repast, so there was zero hesitation when it came time for me to eat. I must have gotten tipsy, because I ate the food without hesitation. This didn't seem like a funeral, so I didn't feel like I was eating at a funeral. In fact, the ambience felt more like a banquet or the prom.

The repast was a nice affair, almost too nice for such a sad event. We celebrated my father's last birthday with a catered sit down dinner but this was nicer than that. Other than his last birthday and the funeral repast, I had never seen so many people get together to celebrate him. It spoke volumes about how we treat the living as opposed to the dead. It shouldn't take death for people to come together to show someone love. Folks always say that but it doesn't seem like anything changes.

I continued to keep my distance from his family to prevent myself from being disrespectful or showing emotion. At an early age, I learned how to keep my feelings to myself. What I didn't learn was how to appropriately and positively process my feelings. Growing up, I didn't trust anyone enough to share them. I also wanted to be as passive-aggressive as possible. When it comes to being passive-aggressive, I can roll with the best of them.

The room was filled with so many people whom I had never seen in my father's presence. They say that funerals are for the living and his definitely was. Most of the people there were friends of the family but not necessarily people who spent much time with him. If he had been surrounded by so much love in life, what a difference it would have made.

My sister and her overnight fiancé sat with Travis and I and two of my very close friends. Yes, we learned at the repast that my sister was engaged to this strange man. I didn't have the mindset to process the information at that moment, so it completely went over my head.

One friend was Brittany, my best friend since high school and the other close friend, Lee, grew up with me. Lee's family and my father's family have been close for many generations. Our families were all connected through multiple friendships and relationships. Lee and I were "play cousins" growing up and became friends as adults. Lee knew just as much about my family as anyone, so she knew what I was dealing with. Throughout the whole ordeal, Lee was a listening ear and someone who was very supportive. The people at my table were the only people that I felt I could trust in the whole room.

The food was pretty good, even better because I had been drinking. My sister complained about the food and then complained about everything else in her life. Sometimes, she could be so childish that you forget she is almost 40 years old. Not only did she find an issue with the food, and the service, she felt the need to share some of her personal sob stories.

After all that, she said she was so sad because she knew that we wouldn't see each other for a long time. Here we go, I thought to myself. She sat at the table and put her pathetic face on, like some victim, as if it was a circumstance beyond her control. My only response to her was, "If you want to see me, come visit me." In other words, I wasn't going to make it my duty to make sure that she and I got to visit one another.

Just as they had before when they tipped the pastor and choir, my father's sisters paid for the banquet and food in a public fashion. Literally, they stood front and center, so everyone could see them. I was under the impression that they had already paid for it earlier in the week. That was one of the reasons that Angela gave when she said she couldn't help with the expenses. Angela said that she and Etta would provide flowers and had paid for the repast.

It wouldn't have mattered if they hadn't helped at all, it was the motive behind it that bothered me and must've bothered them too. They must have felt some guilt for them to keep making such public displays. They knew they hadn't helped with anything but they wanted everyone to think that they had.

Sometime during all the movement, the funeral director made his exit. I figured he would have at least said goodbye after being so accommodating. I also needed to get a letter from him, so Travis would be excused from work.

Angela came to our table to deliver the letter I was in need of. I immediately became suspicious. Why would she have the letter and why would the funeral director give it to her? It was the first time that I was disappointed in the funeral director. I'm sure he didn't think anything of it, but he shouldn't have communicated anything with her or left her responsible for anything.

Eventually we all made our way outside to the patio so that Lee could smoke a cigarette. My sister and her overnight fiancé also wanted to smoke. Even I contemplated smoking a cigarette that day. I quit smoking years ago but I still enjoyed smoke breaks with smokers. You will hear the most interesting stories and learn more about people from going out on a smoke break. There was also something nostalgic about smelling the smoke. Smoking was a part of my life for so long and I was so proud that I had quit. The scent reminded me of just how far I had come and that I had overcome an addiction which was so hard to do.

Etta was already outside smoking when we sat down. She never smoked just one cigarette, so she had probably been out there for quite some time. I hadn't uttered a single word to her since the night she flipped out on Travis and I for leaving, and almost fought Angela. She looked like she felt bad but wasn't ready to talk. I was ready for whatever she had to say that day. I was tipsy, emotional, and fed up. When you're ready for any and everything to be thrown at you, those are the moments when people steer clear of you. Let me have been in a good mood though, it would've been open season for nonsense.

The banquet hall had begun to clear out and folks were stopping by on their way out to wish me well. Angela made sure to invite everyone to her house after the repast. Her party was just beginning. As everyone left, they asked me if they would see me at her house, almost as if they knew I was going to say, "No." There was no way that I was going there.

Lee's aunt, who is also one of Angela's best friends, tried hard to persuade me to show up. She also seemed to know all of my personal business, although I hadn't disclosed much of it to anyone. She asked me about Arizona and then probed me about what my plans were for working when I got back home. When "You're not working, right?" came out, I knew that I had been the topic of another conversation for Angela and everyone in town. I was also sure that the topic of me not working wasn't a positive conversation.

They hadn't talked about me starting over from scratch to pursue dreams. The conversation wasn't about me stepping out on faith or doing what I felt I had been called to do. Their conversation was about me being lazy or even suggesting that I was taking advantage of Travis. I knew Angela all too well and I no longer had any appreciation for her messy, meddling, gossipy ways.

I wasn't rude to Lee's aunt because I knew that she was just making conversation. In her own way, she was dropping hints to let me know that there had been some talking going in. In response, I just tried to drop little hints to let her know that I wasn't going to be dealing with his family any time soon. I made sure to speak loudly when I told people I would not be seen at Angela's house. I wanted Etta to hear me and go back and tell how I was acting.

I got the loudest when I spotted Shay, walking to her car with a bag from the funeral home. She stopped to say goodbye to me, like everyone else and asked me if she would see me later. Before I answered her, I hit her with, "What's that?" I pointed to the funeral home bag. What the hell would anyone be doing with a bag from the funeral home? No one paid a dime to them but me, so why would they have anything. "This is Aunt Irene's bag," she replied. Shay said she was taking it home, since she was leaving early. Irene was still inside though, so why couldn't she carry the bag when she left. "Let me see that," I demanded.

As I looked in the bag, I instantly knew why Angela had delivered the letter Travis needed for work from the funeral home to us earlier. She went through this bag and gave us what she wanted us to have, even though Travis and I had paid the entire bill.

Inside the bag was the DVD from the private viewing with my dad's pictures, the guestbook from the funeral, a framed picture, the cards from the flowers that were sent, and the extra printed materials. She was trying to have Shay sneak out all the things that Travis and I had paid for, thinking that we wouldn't notice. This heifer was stealing, as usual, and was trying to be slick about it.

This was not Irene's bag. This had Angela written all over it. What made her think that she was entitled to anything? It was my father who died and she hadn't contributed anything to the funeral costs. The plan was to make me beg for help with the bill, and now she wanted to take what we had paid for. OH, HELL TO THE NO!

The gloves were all the way off after that. I took the DVD, the guestbook, and cards out of the bag and placed them in the box that the guestbook came in. Again, I made sure that Etta heard me and saw exactly what I was doing. Shay was oblivious, as usual, to what was happening and went on her merry way with an empty bag. Angela had Shay sneak the bag out because she knew that Shay would be clueless about what she was doing. At the same time, Shay was so clueless that she let me take whatever I wanted. The only thing I left in the bag was the picture frame. There was no need for me to take the picture because it wouldn't have fit in my suitcase. Plus, I wanted Angela to see that I had purposely taken what I wanted, and left what I didn't.

Travis, Lee, Brittany, and I left shortly thereafter and headed to a local bar. My sister changed and met us there about an hour later. She showed up with some of our cousins whom I had never even met. She said she had to come and get the the money she needed to drive her and my mother home. If it wasn't for that, I wouldn't have needed her to come back around. She had rubbed me the wrong way earlier in the day, and my attitude sucked really bad in general.

My sister and these new cousins didn't have any money to spend but they were more than comfortable ordering drinks for us to pay for. They reminded me of so many people that I had met in St. Louis, who had no shame in begging or taking advantage of someone who was kind. I knew we were always different but that day it really hit home that my sister and I were worlds apart.

My sister also didn't realize that while she thought her life was so much harder than mine, or that she was so street smart, I had lived on my very own for over 15 years in a city just as rough and tough, if not worse, than where she had been. There was nothing slow about me and I had more street smarts than she thought. She had fooled herself into thinking that I grew up with some silver spoon or that she was the only one of the two of us who knew anything about struggle.

Lee invited some of her girlfriends to the bar, who then invited us to hang out with them afterward. It was the best excuse for my sister and I to go our separate ways. I couldn't invite her to a place that I was invited to, even though I had invited Brittany. Immediately, my sister threw on her sad face and poked her lip out. She was trying to use her victim face again. It didn't work in January and it damn sure didn't work at all on that day, especially after what I had just been through. She was trying to get over on me because she didn't have any money and I didn't want to be bothered. Every family member was trying to drain me at that point. I had no job, had just moved, and my father had just been buried to the tune of $13,000. Yet, no one seemed to care in the least bit about me or my situation.

Hanging out and drinking with Lee and her girlfriends was a much needed distraction that night. I don't know if I was drinking to numb myself from the funeral or numb myself from the betrayal of my father's family. As crazy as my father's family always was, I never expected them to stoop this low.

Just months ago, I had predicted that when my father passed, I would no longer remain in contact with his family. What I hadn't predicted was the nature of our severing ties. I thought that I would just graciously back away and leave them to themselves. At that time, we were on good terms, but I still felt like it was better for me to go my own way. I knew then that I was no longer compatible with the talking behind backs, gossiping, fake concern, and general negativity. It's possible that I would've never been able to fully distance myself had they not been exposed. Still, it doesn't feel good to leave any relationship on bad terms.

When I got back to Phoenix, I was angrier than I had ever been in my life and I actually thirsted for vengeance. As I had done before, I started writing. This time, my writing was filled with anger, my words filled with vengeance. I was going to write about all of it and expose them to the world. My dream of being a writer was now intertwined with getting back at those who had hurt me the most.

In the days that followed, I wrote and I wrote and I cried and cried. I told anyone who would listen about what happened and asked them if I was crazy for feeling the way that I felt. I sought validation for my frustration and anger. Everyone that I spoke with agreed that I had been violated.

None of it helped me. The more that I wrote and convinced myself that I had been wronged, not just recently, but throughout my whole life, the angrier I became. The person who I had worked so hard to become was unrecognizable. There was nothing that made me smile, nothing that soothed my spirit. I couldn't find a place of positivity to refocus myself. My mind raced with all that they had ever done to me, and what could've been of my life had they not been a part of it. I imagined how many other times they had worked together to create a struggle for me. And what about my father! What had they done to him over the years?

I was falling apart and I just continued to become angrier. There weren't enough ways to lash out and express my anger. Nothing provided solace. The entire ordeal was getting the best of me and it was going to take me over, if I continued to let it. Writing didn't release me like it had before.

I began making videos on Facebook, dropping hints publicly about what had been done to me. All I wanted was for all of the people who they had put on such a show for to know who they truly were. No matter how much I lashed out, I found myself back at square one, which only furthered my frustration.

After seeing his family for who they truly were, I understood my father completely. I felt closer to him in death than I ever did when he was alive. He was far from perfect but there were some levels that he wouldn't stoop too. First, he would be upfront with anyone about what he believed was right. To many people, he was rude or disrespectful because he was too upfront at times. However, he would've never plotted against any of his sisters' children, especially not after one of them had died.

The days surrounding his funeral, I got to experience first hand what he had gone through all his life. They were all united against me, covering their tracks, playing games, making sure that I would look crazy if I had called them out on what was really going on. The difference between my father and I was that I didn't feel a need to address them for what they were trying to do. I wasn't going to lash out and continue that generational curse. As long as I knew, it was enough for me.

The last phone conversation that my father and I had, I told him that he should come to Phoenix when he got better. He told me then, that he may have to come to Phoenix for a long time. I believe his spirit came back to Phoenix with us. I placed a picture of him in a picture frame that is decorated with the word "Family."

It was the first time that I ever had placed a picture of my father in my home. The summer before he passed, he told me not to worry about his death because he was going to be my guardian angel. He also told me that he could do more for me from the other side. Those words stuck with me throughout the whole time he was sick and after he passed, it seemed like he did start helping me from the other side.

In the midst of all of my anger and frustration, some unbelievable things happened after we got back to

Phoenix. I received a job offer without trying. It just fell in my lap. I got hired in a furniture store that is only open on weekends. The pay was pretty good, but more importantly, I would still have the rest of the week to work on my writing. Financially, Travis and I were secure but this new job would keep us financially stable and still allow me the time to pursue all of my goals.

Once again, GOD was looking out for me. What seemed like an ongoing cycle of rejection from jobs was actually GOD's plan to keep me on track with what I really wanted to do. GOD was keeping me aligned with the universe.

May 5th was my first day and by the end of my first day, I felt that the job was too good to be true. My only objective was to help customers complete credit applications. For most of the day, I did nothing but wait and wait and wait some more. I had taken six applications at the end of my first day, which combined, couldn't have required me to work more than a total of thirty minutes. The other seven and a half hours, I just sat around and watched the television set that was setup for customer viewing.

My new supervisor was astonished that I had taken six applications in one day. "We did six applications the entire weekend last week!" she exclaimed. I didn't understand what the big deal was, but everyone else was so impressed by the number of applications that I had taken. I asked her how many applications she wanted me to take or if I had any goals. There were none. There were no goals, no quotas, and no pressure on me.

This new job was a complete contrast to the stress and pressure-filled environment of teaching. She told me that some days would be busier than others and that I should find a way to keep myself occupied during my down time. "Bring a book!" she said. I had an even better idea. I would write a book.

After a few weeks, I no longer worried about how long the job would last or whether it was too good to be true. I was just happy that I had been given an opportunity to make such easy money. All I could do was be grateful.

When you operate out of a place of gratitude, the universe responds in magnitudes. I've always appreciated what I've had but there have been times when I had to practice having an attitude of gratitude. This wasn't the case anymore. I didn't have to try to be grateful, I was authentically and easily grateful.

Feeling gratitude for my new job was the first step on the road to my recovery from the anger I had developed after my father's funeral. It was what I needed to begin changing the momentum in my life. All I had been focusing on was my anger up until that point. This new job reminded me that GOD was still in my life and still very much in my corner. As I shifted my energy from negative to positive, I was positioning myself to attract more positivity.

The higher ups for my new employer began lauding me with praise. My performance was both amazing and record-breaking to them. They kept coming to visit, praising me about the improvement in the numbers and how well I spoke and interacted with clients and customers. The district manager made sure to visit while on his trip from Utah to tell me how happy he was with me. I hadn't done anything spectacular and it didn't feel like work at all. It didn't pay as much as my teaching job, but it paid enough and it paid well. More importantly, I spent most of my time at work writing my book. On my days off, I wrote more and relaxed. Travis and I used our days off together to travel and spend time in our new city. He worked hard to see that I enjoyed my life and didn't let negativity take me over. It was paying off and the momentum I was feeling only made me believe that things were only going to get better.

CHAPTER TWELVE: ESTATE TAX

My new job and all of the success that came with it only made me think more good things were on the horizon. I thought of the boy in *The Alchemist* and how he had stumbled upon a job at a crystal shop. The boy knew that working in the crystal shop was not what he wanted to do forever, but he was successful at improving business for the owner of the crystal merchant. The boy had other goals in life, mainly finding treasure, but he had contemplated returning to his former life as a shepherd.

It was the way things were playing out for me as well. I wanted to go after my treasure, but I had contemplated returning to teaching. The boy had done such a good job working in the crystal shop that the merchant was doing better than ever. The crystal shop owner told the boy that the success of his shop was proof that the boy was blessed and brought blessings wherever he went.

That was how things were going for me and my employer also. Eventually, the boy moved on and continued to search for his treasure, after the merchant nudged him not to become complacent as he had. The job served a purpose for the boy for a spell but he was always called back to search for his treasure.

Everything at work continued to be successful which made it easier for me to immerse myself in my writing. As I wrote about family members, there were moments when vengeance re-entered my heart. There was a connection between their recent behavior and the behaviors that they exhibited throughout my entire life. My writing was opening my heart to be completely honest with what I felt, something I had never done before. I had always kept my mouth shut to give the appearance that I hadn't been hurt by others, especially family. As I recalled more and more experiences in my life, I discovered a pattern of hurt. I also discovered a pattern of strength and greatness.

Since I wasn't speaking to anyone in the family, the only person that I could really talk to about the family was Lee. She knew them as much as I did and knew my story. Camille reached out a few times via text messages, but I couldn't tell her much. Angela is her mother, so she wouldn't take my side. Even Kyle remained partial to Angela. I could talk to Kyle about everything, but she always gave Angela a pass. She made it clear that Irene, Mya, and Etta were horrible but she never went all the way there with regard to Angela.

Shay never called but I was friends with her on Facebook, so I saw her post things on a daily basis. I wasn't surprised that I didn't hear from her, she seemed very preoccupied with making YouTube videos on hair and makeup. Shay was lucky. None of what went on seemed to phase her.

I could also find out more dirt talking to Lee. Her aunts were always over Angela's house, soaking up Angela's gossip. Lee told me that the night of my father's funeral, Angela and her guests had a roundtable discussion about me. My father used to joke about Angela's kitchen table being "The Roundtable," since so many locals would congregate there to get the scoop.

Angela, Irene, and Mya were the leaders of the discussion. Disparaging me was the entertainment for the night and they went very low to entertain. Angela told everyone that I had taken out a loan to pay for my father's funeral, trying to insinuate something about my financial situation. It shouldn't have mattered how we paid for the funeral but the fact that she was lying about it to make me look like some kind of loser, made my blood boil. No one offered to help in any capacity, so what did it matter to them. After all they had tried to do to bring me to my knees and beg, they wanted to slander me as well.

It was also an issue for Angela that I took possession of the guestbook that she tried to steal. She wanted to send everyone a thank you card for coming and express gratitude for their donations. I hadn't received a donation from anyone, so what did the donations pay for? I thought that if someone's parent died, and they paid the bill, you would make sure that any monies collected were given to them. In this family, it didn't go that way. They must have paid for the choir's tip or the catering that Angela and Etta said they had paid for. All of the donations were in Angela's possession and she never turned over a penny to me.

I don't know what Angela did with the money but it was of no assistance in paying for the funeral, so I really wasn't concerned about whether she was able to send a thank you card to anyone. Her main concern was saving face and keeping up appearances with the locals. That was on her to figure out since she kept all the money. All she had to do was open all the cards that she had and respond to whomever signed the card. Angela had to really be out of her mind to make herself a victim in this case but it was something she always found a way to do.

Mya told everyone that I had abandoned my father to "chase after a n---a," referring to my relationship with Travis. As I had suspected, they all were salivating over the fact that I had stopped working, as if I had never worked a day in my life. Mya also told them I wasn't working because I was living off of my father's social security check and getting some sort of stipend for being his caregiver. None of it was true, so she had either took the time to concoct a complete lie or she was just stupid. Lee said that the gossip was so bad that her aunts started to defend me, and then left.

Of course, this was all second and third hand information, but the fact that Lee's aunts went back and filled Lee in was proof enough to me that some really hurtful things were being said behind my back. The irony in it all is that while Angela and Mya thought they were bad mouthing me, they only made themselves look bad. No one believed them or even supported them. When Lee's aunts told her what Angela and Mya were saying, they weren't cheering them on but condemning them.

Not only was it hurtful hearing these things repeated to me, it was completely unfair. What had I ever done to any of them, especially Mya? I never liked her but I had never done anything to her. What did she gain from bad-mouthing me on the very same day that my father had been buried? Everyone had pretended to mourn, but they were in good enough spirits to tend to the business as usual of keeping up confusion and negativity.

I couldn't help but feel violated. I had avoided confronting anyone or even being in their presence because I didn't want to lash out. In return, I got trashed all over town; a town that I don't live in, without being able to defend myself. At that point, I was past feeling hurt or angry, I was being disrespected. I was also done with entertaining any shred of doubt whether these bridges needed to be burned, once and for all. The time had come for me to put everything on the table. It wouldn't be lashing out; it would be demanding respect.

I decided that I would call Angela to see if any type of relationship could be salvaged. I had no interest in dealing with Mya. As far as I am concerned, Mya can croak and I will have no feelings about it. I do not wish any bad upon her, but she has placed herself in that irrelevant category in my life.

Angela and I had much more history and I actually had higher expectations for her. For years, she touted herself as a mother figure to me and more recently she boasted that she was the only person who had been there for me in my life. She might have approached the situation like she would with her own children, with understanding, compassion, and maybe even some remorse, if I had gotten lucky. That didn't happen.

I tried to keep the phone conversation respectable. Regardless of whatever issues I faced with the family, I always tried to be respectful and follow those rules about respecting your elders and knowing your place. I tried, but I always seemed to forget those rules very quickly.

The first thing I asked her was "Why are you talking about me and what do you all want from me?" I had done everything that I was supposed to do in the situation. I handled all of my business as it pertained to burying my father. I worked on a relationship with him, in spite of all that had taken place in our past. Still, they chose to tear me apart.

"What are you talking about?" was her reply. Angela used the line of questioning that people use when they are guilty of talking about you and need to stall for time. "You know what I'm talking about!" I asserted. By questioning me, she could buy time and find out what I knew, so she could formulate some form of defense.

She chose to stick with "I don't know what you're talking about." So, I let her know exactly what I was talking about. I went completely down the list of things that I had been told, starting with what she said and ending with what Mya said. "Who told you that?" she inquired. She was still pivoting and deflecting from the issue at hand. It really didn't matter who told me what, and that wasn't the reason that I had called her. "Did you say it?" I asserted. My tone was becoming more aggressive and angry, but I made sure to contain myself. Angela pivoted again. "If you can't tell me who said it, then I can't talk to you about it," she quipped.

What the hell sense did that make? After that, I let her have it and I didn't hold anything back. The only effort I made to not disrespect her was to refrain from cursing at her. Other than that, my tone and approach would've been considered disrespectful according to the respect your elder's standard.

I was more certain everything that Lee told me was true. Angela couldn't even defend herself and she wouldn't own up to anything that she did or said. I hadn't even gone into the issue of the funeral and that she had stolen the donations. I didn't bring up how she tried to steal the guestbook or DVD either. I didn't feel the need to. If that's how she wanted to operate and she felt that entitled, that was on her, but I wasn't going to be trashed or bad mouthed, in addition to everything else they had done.

After I ranted for what seemed like minutes, but was actually only seconds, Angela pivoted in a different direction, but still continued to deflect from the issue. "I stood up for you when everyone was talking about you!" she exclaimed. She had pivoted from denying or deflecting to throwing people under the bus. "You should've never allowed a conversation like that at your house!" I fired back. It was my attempt to invoke some sense of loyalty from her. "You're just mad because your dad is dead!" she replied. It was a new low, among many lows, and an indicator that there wouldn't be any resolution for the grievances that I aired.

So much for my thinking that Angela actually valued our relationship. "I'm not upset about my father being dead, I'm ok with it," I asserted. "Well, I guess you said what you have to say. You have a nice life," she responded. That was the end of the conversation.

To Angela, I had done the unthinkable. I had opened my mouth and called her out. There was really no consideration of how I felt. The way that she ended the conversation only confirmed all that I had been thinking for months about the conditions that were placed on me, if I wanted to be loved by his family. Angela saw no value in me or my feelings. She wouldn't miss me. She had kept me around as long as I pretended that everything was fine between us. The moment I raised a genuine issue, was the moment that ended it all. Just like that, I was dismissed out of her life. That's not how love works.

How could it be so easy just to say goodbye to someone who you claim you love, someone that you claim was like a child to you? It was so easy to just move on without me and all because I stood up for myself against the things that she had said about me.

I wasn't worthy of an apology, instead I was wrong for speaking up and she was a victim once again. After it was all over, I felt like I hadn't said enough. I wished that I had said everything, all that I had ever felt, about them all. Talking to Angela didn't provide me with any relief. I was still reeling with hurt, frustration, and anger.

I regretted that I hadn't said anything about their plan to make me beg. I put together a group text message, and took screenshots of the checks that Travis and I had written for the payment of the funeral. I wanted them all to know that I knew about their plan. I also wanted them to know that Travis had helped me, and was the only person who had helped me. He wasn't just some "n---a", as Mya had referred to him, that I was chasing after. Travis loved me and had been there for me in my time of need, when they weren't.

Mya was the only one to respond to the group message. It was so obvious that she had some sort of personal vendetta against me. I was so glad that she chose to say something. I had been waiting for her to come for me again. I thought I had owed her one before, but this time I was ready to inflict some injuries to her, just as she had to me. She was far from perfect and thanks to her new bestie Angela, the same aunt that she sat up and trashed me with, I knew a lot about her that she didn't know I was aware of.

I composed a text message about Mya's affair with a married man. I knew that I was reaching just as low as they were but I didn't care anymore. I just wanted to hurt Mya the same way that I had been hurt. It still wouldn't catch me up to the hurt that they had caused me, but it was a start.

Every mean thing I had ever heard about Mya, I typed in the text and sent it out to everyone. I used the same group text recipient list that we used when we were texting about my father when he was in the hospital. I called Mya names, brought up her promiscuity, and even talked about her acne. I hadn't forgot how insecure she was about her skin, just weeks earlier. Mya tried to respond but she was no match for me. I was willing to go as low as I could to make my point. I was so hurt that I had no regard for civility. I knew that I was wrong and that nothing good was going to come from being mean or taking the low road but I couldn't stop.

Within minutes of it all ending, I broke into tears and felt very sharp pains shooting through my chest. I was so disappointed in myself at how I had carried on. I knew what people meant when they talked about getting out of character. I had worked so hard to be a positive person and a good person that the negativity and negative behavior took a physical and mental toll on me. I didn't feel good at all but I didn't want to take any of it back either.

As I cried, I had a revelation about who I was and the direction my life was going. I had let these people take me back yet again, this time even further to a level of negativity that I had long ascended from. Being mean and malicious brought me zero satisfaction. Years before, I would've engaged in the name calling and combat with pleasure. I would've secretly desired for it to continue and escalate. That was no longer the case for me anymore, I had become a believer of GOD and my behavior went against GOD because I had been disrespectful and malicious towards another human being. Stooping to their level meant I was moving in the wrong direction and I was totally out of alignment with who I was. Mya, Angela, Etta and Irene were stuck way back there where I had moved so far away from.

The longer that you live, the things you learn and store begin to make sense. The situation made me think of the bible verse Luke 23:34, "Forgive them father, for they know not what they do." My father's family were who they were because of what they had lived. They didn't know any better. That bible verse had always been a principle that I wished I was good enough to embrace. There I was, actually understanding it wholeheartedly.

GOD knows, I didn't really want to forgive them and I didn't really think it was possible for me to forgive them. It was going to eat me up, if I didn't, as hating them had eaten me up for so many years before. It just seemed so much more difficult to forgive them for a second time when it took me years to forgive them the first time. I knew that I had to try, even if I didn't succeed at first. So I took the first step.

The truth is, I wasn't really sorry and I didn't really know how I was going to forgive them. I actually felt that it was impossible to forgive them for what they had done, especially when I thought about it all in the context of everything they had ever done. So, I asked GOD to forgive me and show me the way forward. I drafted another group text in which I apologized for my comments and my behavior. I didn't really mean it but I figured it was the first step in what was going to be many in trying to get past where I was. Getting beyond my anger and rage towards them was going to be one of the hardest challenges in my life. I had done it before though, and I knew that I could do it again.

The best thing for me at the time was to remove them from my life completely. I went through my phone and blocked all of their phone numbers so that they couldn't contact me. If they had sent me a message or called, it would've just reignited all of the flames in me that I was trying to extinguish. I went through my Facebook friends list and deleted all of them. Each time I looked at their posts, I thought they were trying to send subliminal messages towards me. If it wasn't that, I would just get disgusted by seeing them on there smiling and being happy. I couldn't stand to see them or have any connection. It felt like a petty move, but I had to prevent myself from seeing their posts and pictures.

Angela beat me to it and blocked me before I was able to block her. Apparently, she must have felt the same way about me that I felt about her. In this day and age, getting blocked on social media is the ultimate dismissal. I had deleted them as friends, but she blocked me altogether, which sends a much more aggressive message.

I had never felt so strongly about disliking people and it didn't make me feel good at all. One day, I just sat and cried, trying to figure out why I felt this way. All I wanted was to be like I was just a few months before but I couldn't get myself back on track. The feelings were so strong and overwhelming at times that I was convinced that I had developed hatred in my heart. Hate would consume more of me as each day passed.

Confronted with the choice of reverting back to a bitter and unhappy me or becoming stronger than I was before, I created a game plan to try and move myself forward. The first thing I had to do was stop talking about what had happened. I am one of those people who believe that talking about your feelings is beneficial to healing. The only problem that I had was that my talking tended to turn into dwellings. When it came to things I was passionate about, I could talk infinitely and passionately. The fact that I was hurt, and no one involved was working to quell my pain meant that I would stay hurt. In this case, talking about it was only going to perpetuate more hurt. I had to refocus my life on where I wanted to go and not where I had been.

Going forward, I made sure that my conversations were only about the future that I wanted. My next priority was to put my emotions in check. If I could control my emotions, it was the first step to controlling my thoughts. Whenever I began to feel bad about what had happened, I would empower myself by thinking about all that I had overcome in my life. I began constantly reminding myself of who I had become and how I had become this person. The universe had worked in my favor to bring me love, happiness, and success, and I was going to have to get back in touch with it. The hardest part was being disciplined in controlling my emotions, but I had to. I had to stop thinking about everything that had happened. The rest of my life depended on it.

Instead of lashing out when I was angry, I decided to write it all down. That was going to channel my anger into productivity. Feeling productive is a positive emotion, so it was another way for me to actively work at controlling my emotions. What I was writing didn't fit into *From Scratch* or anything I had written before, and I questioned why I was even writing it. I had no idea how I would even use what I had written, or if I could use it at all.

As I read back what I was writing it was depressing and full of victimization. That was not what I wanted my story to be, but it was. Writing about it was putting me back in the same energy space that I was working so hard to distance myself from. That's when it hit me again. BE STILL. Stop writing. If writing was putting me where I didn't want to be, then I should stop.

I stopped talking about what had happened, thinking about what had happened, and now I had stopped writing about what had happened. I went on with life and waited for my next cue from the universe.

It came quick.

A letter arrived, addressed to myself and my father's estate. I hadn't set up an estate for my father when he passed, so I wondered how they located me. The letter said that my father was named as a beneficiary on Aunt Diane's life insurance policy but had not collected on it before he passed. Therefore, the money that was benefited to him, would be benefitted to me.

Whoa!

I had to read it over a few more times to make sure that I was reading it correctly. This was my sign. After all that we had went through to bury my father, I was going to be handsomely rewarded. The policy belonged to Aunt Diane, and just like she had done all my life, she was hooking me up. A part of me downplayed the letter and another part of me thought big. It could've been nothing, but what if it was thousands of dollars. I had to at least find out. The fact that it was Aunt Diane's policy was a sign to me because she always treated me like I was someone special. It was just like all those Christmas visits that she made when I was a child. She was showing up at the last moment but bringing a bit of cheer and maybe even that gift that I had asked for but didn't get!

CHAPTER THIRTEEN: INSURANCE POLICY

I faxed a copy of my father's death certificate to the insurance company as requested, hoping that they would tell me how much the benefit was for. At least then, I would know whether it was worth going after. No such luck. The insurance company wouldn't provide me with any information on the amount of the insurance policy because an estate had not been established yet. In order for me to even find out how much it was worth, I was going to have to do a lot of work.

The first thing I would have to do is get my mother to sign off on a form of renunciation, so that I could be the administrator of his estate. It was all so intimidating that it stressed me out right from the start. Not to mention, all of the new vocabulary and terminology that I had to learn. After she signed off, I would have to register an estate in the county my father lived in when he died. That meant I would have to go to Virginia to meet with my mother, then go to New Jersey to file paperwork to be named the administrator of my father's estate. All of this had to be done before I could even find out how much the benefit was worth.

On one hand, I felt like the joke was going to be on me. I was going to travel up and down the eastern seaboard just to end up with a couple hundred dollars. On the other hand, I felt like GOD had given me the biggest sign yet and that I would be blessed just for stepping out on faith. Anything was possible. Just what if Aunt Diane had left my dad a ton of money? She was so proud of the family and our name that maybe she had left him a nice inheritance, which was going to be transferred to me!

The least I could do was find out, even if that meant taking a loss. There was no way that I could have went on without knowing. So, I made the arrangements to go on this mission, not knowing what the outcome would be. I was acting completely on faith, knowing that GOD was watching me.

My first stop would be Richmond, VA, where my mother lived. I had to figure out how to approach her with the news. Legally, she was entitled to anything that belonged to my father after his death. Of course, he had just minor possessions but this policy might have been worth something. I wondered if she would want to get her hands on some of it. While she was entitled legally, I felt more entitled because I had paid so much to bury him. At that point, I just wanted to feel that I wasn't going to keep getting screwed over by everyone.

I prayed about it and asked GOD to guide my steps. It was revealed to me that what GOD has for me, is for me, and nothing that anyone was going to do could prevent me from receiving what HE had intended for me. So, I called her and let her know that there was some money out there for one of us and it was up to her to decide whether I would go and get it or she would go and get it.

Either she figured there was going to be a lot of work involved or she really felt that I deserved whatever it was because she opted out. "You deserve whatever it is, after all that you've had to do," she said. It was the response that I had hoped she would give. It was the first time since my father had passed that someone had considered *my* best interest. Her only request was that I gave her a copy of my father's death certificate so that she could submit it to the social security office. Both my mother and father had been receiving disability payments for years and now she was able to receive his after his death. I agreed to bring her a copy and she agreed to sign over rights of administration to me.

The logistics to my mission made it all the more challenging. The entire experience seemed like a mission or operation because it really did require a lot of planning and coordination. I can never say anything bad about the internet because I wouldn't have been able to get most of it done without my iPhone and Google.

We only had two days to get it all done before we had to head back to Phoenix for Travis to go to work. We left on a Tuesday night at midnight and arrived in Richmond at 8:00 AM the next morning. Our flight required us to switch planes in Detroit, so we spent more time traveling than what we would've liked, but Richmond is not the kind of place that you can easily get a non-stop flight to, unless you're coming from somewhere on the East Coast. We rented a vehicle at the Richmond airport and made our way to meet with my mother, along with a notary.

Virginia brought back many memories of my childhood and my late young adulthood. My mother had custody of me in the summers, so I spent my summers there with her. When I was 18, I moved to Virginia from St. Louis for a brief two months. It was the first time that I had been back to Richmond since 2002. At that time, Kyle had just bought her house and I felt like I was such a burden. So, I left and went to live with my mother, assuming I would be welcomed with open arms, after so many years of living with my father.

I looked for jobs in Richmond but didn't have any luck. My situation was so desperate that I took a job selling knockoff perfume on the streets. It was part of a scam operation that preyed on people who wanted to make a better life for themselves, like me. We were never paid for working and the only money we made was the money we made off selling the perfume. Everyone sold as much as they could because you were promised your own independent distribution office, which basically meant you would operate your own scam operation. Of course, none of it worked out, and my mother suggested that I go back to

St. Louis. She always insisted that my life would be better, if I stayed with my father and his family. After just two months, I went back to St. Louis.

Life was very different with my mother whenever I visited. She was more emotionally supportive than my father or anyone in his family but she lived in poverty. She didn't work and her only income came from money she would make from singing at church or playing the piano. Other than that, we lived off of food stamps and welfare payments. My father wasn't wealthy by any means, but he did work and living with him provided a more stable environment financially.

Virginia reminded me of those experiences of poverty and how badly I wanted to live a better life. It felt good to return in the financial position that I was in, almost like a redemption of sorts. I am far from rich but in comparison to those days when there was barely any food, I could appreciate how far I had come. Unfortunately, my mother and sister were still living in the very same poverty that they had been in since I was a kid.

My mother rented a small duplex, just blocks from where she had lived for many years. My mother is the type of person who is weary of venturing out or straying from her comfort zone. She moved to Virginia when I was three years old and has lived in the same one-mile proximity the entire time but in different places. Her new place was dated and in disrepair, but affordable. An odor of water damage, or oldness permeated the air. All of the windows were covered up completely and darkness filled the entire place.

It said a lot to me that she did so much to keep out the light. It was as if she had embraced darkness for so long that she shunned the light. Her living area was cluttered with knick-knack items, obsolete VHS tapes, and various sets of furniture. She always crammed a lot of her belongings into a tiny space, as if she was incapable of letting anything go.

Travis and I visited with my mother before we made our way to meet with the notary. The topic of the funeral and my father's family was still fresh on her mind. She asked me if I had spoken with any of them, to which I asserted that I had nothing else to say. I told her about the conversation that Angela and I had and the gossip that Lee shared with me. My mother drew parallels to her wedding day and said that Angela and my grandmother opened all of her wedding gifts without her permission. It was just like how Angela had kept all the funeral donations and tried to steal the items from the funeral home.

My mother had never been their favorite person but she had never spoken of them in the manner that they had spoken of her. She always talked of how mean they were to her but she never really talked about them in a negative way. Travis was interested in hearing more from her, so he asked her what had happened so many years ago. He already knew some of the history between my mother and I but he must have wanted to hear her version.

I heard my mother's story many times before but I listened again. This time, I was able to listen with an ear of discernment. My father always told me that my mother didn't want me. My mother always had a different story. She said my father took custody of me just to spite her. I never thought my mother was lying but I didn't feel that there was any excuse for letting someone take your child, as she said had happened. For most of my childhood, I didn't know what to believe and I as I grew older, I still didn't have a clear understanding.

My mother said that my father never pressed the issue of being a custodial parent. He was content with picking me up on weekends and holidays or spending time with me after school. Basically, he was the kind of father that most kids have when their parents break up and that would've been perfectly acceptable.

She stated that she moved to Virginia with my

sister and I after she went through some serious issues with her own family. As an adult, she came out and told her family that she had been molested by her grandfather. Some of her sisters said the same thing happened to them, but the allegation tore her family apart. She skipped town and decided to start over in Virginia, from scratch.

The next part of her story is where things were always fuzzy to me. After the move, I became very sick and there was nothing that she could do to help me get better. She says that she contacted my father in New Jersey for him to come and get me because she didn't have any medical insurance. My grandmother and Angela showed up instead. They took me to New Jersey and a few weeks later, she was served with custody papers. So, if my father never wanted custody of me, whose idea was it to take my mother to court for custody? It sounded to me like it was Angela and my grandmother's idea.

Even after that, she says that my father didn't show up for court appearances or express interest in being a custodial parent. It wasn't until they finally met up in court and she signed the wrong papers that she realized she had signed over her custodial rights. Her characterization of Angela and my grandmother seemed to align perfectly with what I knew of them. I knew for a fact how very capable of doing things out of spite Angela was and my grandmother left a lasting impression on many that she was mean.

As my mother continued to tell her story, I realized that the reason why I couldn't believe my mother's story or my father's story was because there were more people involved than just the two of them. Finally, I could make more sense of what happened because I now had more pieces to the puzzle. My grandmother and Angela had involved themselves in my father's entire life, and apparently, they had involved themselves in taking me from my mother.

Whenever my grandmother spoke about my

mother, she claimed that I was in my father's custody because my mother wasn't a good caregiver. Yet, everything that they said about my mother never made sense to me. My mother was poor, but she kept a clean house, cooked meals for us, and she loved me. Angela always co-signed what my grandmother said, and more recently she asserted that **both** my mother **and my father** had never been there for me. Of course, it was only after she had fallen out with him that she felt the need to condemn him as a parent.

Everything made so much sense all of a sudden. Just as my father's family had meddled in our relationship, they had meddled in my mother and father's relationship. Taking me from my mother was their idea, not his.

Growing up, I had a front row seat to watching them steamroll his entire life, diminish him as a man, and interfere in all of his business. They did it, time after time, again and again. Maybe, that's why my father was so distant with me as a child. He never really wanted to be a single father. It's possible that he resented me because I was a reminder of who they were forcing him to be, and that he had no control. As long as he had to take care of me, he believed he would need them, and they would always retain control of him.

Was it possible that my grandmother and Angela broke up any family that my father would have outside of them and broke each and every one of us in the process? That's what I felt in my heart of hearts, but I was not prepared to accept it. As much as I felt I had a revelation, the accusation was so intense that it gave me great pause. I didn't let my mother completely off the hook yet, but her story touched me for the first time. It was big step for me and my feelings toward her.

We all headed out to a Chipotle not far from my mother's house. The notary brought her baby with her and ended up sitting with us for quite a while. It was as if we had known her for quite some time as opposed to meeting her for the very first time that day. She earned a nice piece of change that day for stamping a bunch of papers and bragged about how she's able to make money on her own terms while taking care of her children.

My mother and the notary talked about having children and how different two children could be, with my mother drawing a parallel to my sister and I. My mother always said that I was a much easier child to raise than my sister was, to which the notary talked about her older child being a handful as well. That conversation led to a conversation about my sister in general, including where her overnight fiancé came from. That relationship had since ended but my sister found herself in another unhealthy relationship with someone who was friends with the guy she had brought to the funeral. I remembered how badly I wanted to be loved and how I put myself in situations that were no good for me, but never to the extent that my sister had. She needed something that no man could give to her. She needed love, but it was love for herself.

My mother also told me that my sister had swindled me after the funeral. She didn't need the gas money that I gave her to drive back to Virginia, but she took it anyway. My mother had already secured enough money to pay for their entire trip. The church that my mother attends took up an offering to pay for their transportation.

I was irritated and somewhat livid at my sister, but at the same time I was numb. I wasn't surprised but I was disgusted that my sister had used me after she knew all that I was going through at the time. The news was also confirming that I didn't have to feel bad about the distance between my sister and I. We were related, but cut from two very different cloths.

My mother had never eaten Chipotle before and seemed to be tickled and impressed by the entire experience. She had more in common with my father than she probably realized. Both of them had missed out on so many experiences that many of us take for granted, like eating Chipotle. My father got around a bit more than she did but he still had shut himself off from the world quite a bit. That's why I was so surprised to hear of my father's travels during his funeral.

My mother just seemed to be content with very little and had very little drive to experience anything new or different. I thanked GOD that I hadn't inherited their complacency or fear from either of them. As we left the restaurant, I remember her saying "This has been such a really nice visit."

After we dropped my mother back off at home, we left for New Jersey. What was supposed to be a four-hour drive up I-95 ended up being much longer than we had anticipated. The combination of rain and lack of sleep made the drive seem endless. Travis and I napped for a few hours on the flight but we had both been up all day prior to that. Travis fell asleep no less than 30 minutes out of the Richmond city limits. Normally, he would never fall asleep while I was driving on a road trip. We have an agreement that we have to stay awake while the other is driving. This time, he couldn't hold out and I had many hours on the road to think, mainly about my mother and all of the new revelations I had regarding my childhood.

We sat in traffic for most of the ride, making the trip almost seven hours. Driving through Maryland and D.C. during rush hour wasn't in the original plan but we had overstayed our time with my mother in Richmond. The time was worth it and I felt like we had made major progress. I felt good about it too.

It felt strange going to Jersey and knowing that I would not be visiting with any of my father's family. I hadn't even bothered to contact them to let them know we were coming. I was serious about keeping my distance and

I didn't want them to know that I was there, especially since I was there to see if I was inheriting some money. There was no guarantee that they wouldn't try to sabotage me, so I kept mum about the entire situation.

It was unseasonably cold and rainy for June in Jersey, which put a damper on our arrival. Dressed in bright colors, sneakers and shorts, we were immediately bummed by the barely 70-degree weather and rain puddles.

Our first stop in Jersey was Me & U's pizzeria. The silver lining to Jersey is the food. No matter how long it takes to drive or how far you fly, the food makes you forget about any obstacles. I had managed to get Travis hooked on Me & U's chicken cheesesteaks the last few times we visited my father. My father loved Me & U's cheesesteaks too. We had taken him there for his birthday, which turned out to be his last. Because of that, going to Me & U's had a deeper sentimental value than before. We didn't sit down and reminisce though, all we wanted to do was get food, get to our room, and get some rest.

The cold and wet weather persisted well into the next morning. The plan was to get out first thing in the morning and get to the courthouse to get the paperwork that I needed. My nerves were shot that morning. I kept thinking that something was going to go wrong and we would have come all this way for nothing. I always tend to get uncomfortable when I have to deal with courts or governmental agencies. It seems like there is always something that they ask for that you don't have or just when you think you've jumped through all the hoops, there's another hoop, dipped in gasoline, and set ablaze for you to jump through.

Travis did his best to reassure me that everything would go smoothly but I still had some trepidation. We loaded our rental vehicle up for our trek and made our way to the courthouse in the cold and rain, dressed like we belonged back in Phoenix.

The courthouse stands right next door to my high school and I walked past it nearly everyday of my high school years. Never had I stepped foot in the court building and never thought that I would have to. Yet, here I was, some 15 years after leaving town, going into the Gloucester County Court building, in Woodbury, NJ to set up an estate for my deceased father. It was just the latest surreal moment in a string of surreal moments.

Before I made the trip, I did as much research as possible to make sure that I filled out the correct paperwork and followed the appropriate procedures. I looked up the laws of intestate and made sure that my mother signed nearly every affidavit that they could possibly ask for. I wanted to make sure that I was knowledgeable and prepared for whatever may have been thrown at me.

For much of my life in Woodbury, I was subjected to unfair treatment and bullying, so I equated the town with years of unhappiness and frustration. I had held onto so much resentment for the town that I just knew that I was going to encounter some type of small town nonsense. The situation was already frustrating and the last thing I wanted was to lose my temper and snap out on somebody at this courthouse. It wasn't the best mode of thinking but it was the way that I had always approached the town.

We parked the car about a block away from the courthouse and the school. As we walked past the storefronts and law offices, the small town charm impressed me. As a teenager, I couldn't wait to run as far away from this place, but as a man, I could understand why people would live here and raise children. I was all grown up. Perhaps it was all the work that I had done on myself, or my relationship that I had developed with GOD. Maybe it was dealing with the death of my father. It could have been a combination of it all but I was thinking like a grown man, and I recognized it in myself.

My business was in the surrogate's office. The

entrance to the office was around the back of the courthouse. Security checked us and made us dump our coffee cups before entering. I must admit, I didn't expect such formalities for a small town. The office wall was hidden by records stacked up to the ceiling. The room contained so much history.

I wanted to take one of the record books out and just smell it to see if it had that smell that old library books have. There was no telling what was contained in all these records. I thought about life's benchmarks and how we feel like the first person to reach them when it's our turn. Numerous people had done the very same thing that I was there to do that day.

There were four cubicles on the right side facing the windows, and a long counter for record reading splitting the office into two sections. A very informal waiting area with two chairs faced the row of cubicles. We waited for a few minutes before a tall woman with big hair rose from behind her cubicle. Immediately, I noticed her jewelry and makeup. This woman was dedicated to her appearance. She had a ring on every one of her fingers and a skirt that floated with the slightest movement. You could tell that she actually woke up in the morning and put effort into what she wanted to look like.

The woman's smile was intoxicating and her tone was inviting. Immediately, I could tell that she was extremely nice and pleasant. "Come on back," she said as she signaled us toward her. We followed without hesitation. I looked around her cubicle and noticed that she had decorated it with pictures of her family, flowers, and high heel figurines. Then, I noticed a letter hanging that someone had written to her. It was from a woman who had lost her husband and had worked with her to set up an estate. The letter detailed how helpful she had been and how her sense of humor had made such a tough situation easier. I thanked GOD that he had put someone like her in this position because I knew that she had helped so many more people get through dealing with the death of a loved one.

I also noticed a drawer full of high heels in all kinds of colors and prints. She also wore a pair on her feet. Some of her fashion choices were questionable but her shoes were on point.

"You like shoes?" I asked. She burst into laughter. "I love shoes, you should see my car and my closet. Those are just my emergency pairs." she responded. "Emergency pairs?" I inquired. "I usually change out of those when I leave and put on some different ones to wear home," she added.

This woman made me forget about why I had even come there. I just wanted to talk about shoes after that. A calm and a peace came over me, not just about the day, but about everything that had happened in the months that preceded. This woman was a truly good person that I had come across and I appreciated her energy. I knew that everything was going to be okay.

CHAPTER FOURTEEN: FAMILY VALUES

I can't remember her name but I remember her high heel shoes. She left an impression on me that I will never forget. "What brings you in today?" she asked with a welcoming smile. It was such a simple question but I had almost forgot about the mission we were on after talking about shoes. I explained to her my situation and that I had come all the way from Phoenix. She seemed generally excited about the prospects that I could be getting a large sum of money. "Well, let's see what we can do to help you!" she said, as she turned to her computer. Any anxiety I had was gone at that point. Just one nice person made me feel that maybe Woodbury wasn't such a bad place. Maybe it was just my experiences.

I pulled out my file folder full of signed and notarized documents and laid them out. The lady with the high heel shoes smiled and nodded in approval. "Awesome, you have everything that we're going to need. You sure are thorough" she said. In that moment, I was proud of myself for taking care of my business. She began typing in my information to start up a new file.

As she typed, I noticed my grandmother's name come up in the system when she entered in my last name. An estate for my grandmother was in the system as well. She hadn't left anything behind, so what was the purpose of establishing an estate for her, and who had set one up? I didn't give it much thought, I figured someone had gone through the process as a formality.

When my grandmother died, she was cremated and we held a memorial service at the graveyard. Eventually, her remains were interred on top of the lot that my grandfather was buried in. Her services were conducted by the same funeral home as my father but they were much less expensive. In fact, the entire approach to her burial was much different than the way my father's burial was approached. There was no fancy repast or extravagant private viewing. The funeral home let us see her before her cremation but the viewing was provided as a courtesy. When my father's sisters were footing the bill, they took a much different approach.

I wondered what my grandmother's estate was comprised of and who was the administrator. When I was researching the process for setting up an estate for my father, I learned a lot about the intestate laws in New Jersey. There were certain steps necessary depending upon what a person was leaving behind and whether or not they had left a will. I didn't have to follow all of the steps to set up an estate for my father because he didn't own any property or leave a will. An executor was not required and I was only required to setup an administrator, so that I could close any bank accounts, remove any personal property, or as in this case, receive any payments sent to him after his death.

The house that my father lived in before he died had never been transferred to his name, and it had never been transferred to my grandmother's name either before she had passed. The house was still in my grandfather's name, who passed away days after my third birthday. My grandmother's estate wouldn't have differed much from my father's. She didn't own any property or have an insurance policy either. Nobody received anything as an inheritance, so what was the estate for? The only reason I was setting one up was because there was money out there. Maybe there was some money out there when my grandmother died and I just didn't know about it. I wasn't there to figure out anything surrounding my grandmother's passing, so I refocused myself on what I had come there to do, but I did take note.

The lady with the high heels asked me for a list of my father's assets. I figured he had a few dollars in his bank account and some personal items such as electronics and clothing. She asked me about the insurance policy that listed him as a beneficiary, but I told her I couldn't find out how much it was worth. She said that she had to have the amount in order to determine how much his estate was actually worth, to determine what steps would be necessary. If the policy had a substantial worth, I would have to get a surety bond for the worth of his estate. The bond would make sure that I paid off all of his debts with whatever assets he had.

I couldn't tell her how much the policy was worth because I couldn't get the information from the insurance company. The insurance company wouldn't give me the information because I didn't have a court order. I couldn't get the court order from her without declaring how much the insurance policy was worth. It seemed as if we were about to go in circles but the ladies at the court were understanding, and surprisingly helpful. "Let me see what I can find out," said the lady in the high heels. "Sometimes, they'll give us some information, if I say I'm from the court," she added and followed with a wink.

The lady with the high heels got on the phone with a representative at the insurance agency. She smiled and used terms of endearment to work her magic. It was as if she was waiting on someone on the other end to slip up and spill the beans. As I listened to her sweet tone, I could only admire her tact and approach. They say you get more bees with honey, and that summed up her entire approach. I made a note to self to be more like the lady in the high heels whenever I found myself in a precarious situation. The representative almost fell for it but backed away at the last second. They were not going to tell us how much the policy was worth until the court filed the court order.

The back and forth between the court and the insurance company only increased the speculation on my behalf. It must be a lot, I thought to myself. If it weren't a lot, they wouldn't be being so secretive. I thought about what I was going to do if it were a lot. I was going to directly invest it into my dreams. I was going to build an empire with my family name using the money that was bestowed to me by the only other people who shared my name. It was poetic justice that money from my great-aunt was inherited by my father, and then inherited by me. After what my father's sisters had tried to do, I was justified in keeping it all to myself. This may have been my great reward for doing the right thing.

The lady with the high heels solicited the help of her co-worker in the next cubicle over. This woman was completely different than the lady in the high heels. She didn't use as much honey as the lady with the high heels, but she had the same amount of finesse. Her method relied on the law of averages. She would keep calling and talk to as many people at the insurance company until someone just gave up the information

I stared at her pen as it touched a piece of paper lying on her desk. I thought that she was going to write the amount down on the paper at any moment. She started to write but it wasn't a number. Then, she handed me the phone. They were only going to share the amount with me. Her approach had worked.

By now, the lady in the high heels and her co-worker were just as invested in finding out the amount as I was. We were all wondering what was in store for me or whether I had made this trip in vain. I placed the phone to my ear and a woman with a strong Philadelphia accent greeted me. I knew the accent from growing up so close to Philadelphia. The correspondence from the insurance company came from a Philadelphia address and they had Philadelphia phone number.

"$591" said the voice on the phone. Really, I thought. I paused. It felt like an hour had passed in a ten second time frame. It was secretly what I had anticipated. While I dreamed of it being more, I was only trying to be positive. Deep down inside, I didn't actually expect to get rich here. "Okay, Thank You," I said in my most underwhelming voice. There was nothing else to say anymore and I hung up the phone. "What'd they say?" asked the court clerk. "$591," I said and immediately burst out into laughter. The court clerk's face dropped. "Well, at least you know," she added. "Thanks for all your help," I said and returned to the lady with the high heel's cubicle.

"Well, we're just going to give you an administrator's order since it's such a small amount. You won't need to get a surety bond," said the lady in the high heels. "That's too bad," she added. "But you never know what else could come your way. And you did the right thing. You found out."

I should've been disappointed but I wasn't for some reason. There was nothing else that could have disappointed me after all that I had been through recently. I was actually content with knowing that I had tried. Plus, the lady in the high heels was right. Who knew what the future held for me? This wasn't the end. I had stepped out on faith and whenever you do that, GOD responds. There was definitely going to be more to this story.

We gathered the documents and headed to the rental car. Travis didn't say anything but he looked like he wanted to say a bunch or burst out into laughter. He more than likely assumed that I was very upset, so he kept quiet. "It's ok," I said, letting him know that I wasn't upset. Then, I let out a giggle. He burst out into laughter. "At least you know, you had to find out," he said. It was really the only consolation that I or anyone could give to myself. I just kept maintaining this feeling that something more was going to come from this trip, regardless of how disappointing it seemed.

We drove directly across the street to a branch of my father's bank. It wasn't part of the original plan, but I figured that there may have been some money left in his account. Since we had this court order, I figured I would follow all of the steps that I read about online. Plus, I could now be held liable for any debt incurred by his estate. At the most, I expected there to be $200 in his account. That's the amount that I put on the list of his assets that I turned over to the court.

I showed the teller the court order and asked her to close the account. The teller told me she couldn't close the account because it was overdrawn. Figures, I thought to myself. "How much is it overdrawn?" I asked, thinking it would be a few dollars. This man's bill seemed to keep getting bigger and bigger, I thought to myself. I had just paid to get the court order and now I had to pay to close this bank account. The teller notified me that the account was overdrawn to the tune of nearly $3,000. I gasped. How could his account be overdrawn? He had been dead for over two months.

The teller printed out a transaction history dating back to January. The account was in good standing up until April 19, just days after his passing. The first overdraft occurred when his debit card was used to pay someone's mortgage and satellite subscription bill. Either his debit card had been stolen or it was being used by someone who had access to it. I couldn't believe my eyes. Who would have had access to his checking account information or debit card? That's when the light bulb went off! The only people who had access to them were his sisters. If what I was thinking turned out to be true, it was going to be the most substantial and final confirmation that I would ever need.

I looked further on into the statements and saw the fraudulent activity had continued for the next two months. Two more social security checks had been direct deposited into his bank account after he had passed. The thief had paid their mortgage once again, ordered close to $80 worth of chicken wings from a takeout joint, and wrote four checks. Two of the checks cleared and two bounced.

The social security checks that were deposited had brought the account back from being overdrawn but the checks that were written were well over the amount available in the account and again caused the account to be overdrawn into the thousands. All in all, someone had pocketed almost $4,000 as a result of the activity.

My gut feeling was that one of his sisters was responsible. It was the same gut feeling that I had went back and forth with throughout the entire time he was hospitalized. I didn't want to accept that one of his sisters would use his death for their own personal gain. I also didn't want to believe that after all the money we had spent for the funeral, there would be no consideration for our financial situation. However, I couldn't put it past them after the way they had behaved.

Still, I didn't want to completely accept that one of his sisters would stoop so low. It was like the bar just kept getting lower and lower. If one of them had access to his bank account, why wasn't any of the money offered to help us with the expenses? Instead, not even 3 days after his funeral, the money in his account was being used to pay for mortgages, satellite television, and enough chicken wings to feed a party.

Fortunately, the bank manager was willing to waive all of the over drafted items and closed the account. He advised me to file a police report to get to the bottom of things. The bank manager could not give me any information as to who the checks were written to and so forth. If a detective was involved, the bank would have to divulge everything to the police. I wanted to know answers, so I heeded his advice.

I knew it wasn't Etta, she was very financially stable and it didn't fit her character. Irene and Angela lived in the same proximity and both of them had done things like this before. Irene herself had spoken about her financial situation in negative terms recently. When Irene and I were close, I remembered her having issues trying to open a bank account because of irresponsible activities. She had become big on church, so I hoped that it wasn't her. Still, I didn't put it past her.

Angela was my prime suspect for no other reason than she was greedy and always trying to find a way to get over. She was fired from her job last year after they found out that she had been stealing from them for the 17 years that she worked there. The charges on the account also seemed to point directly to Angela as well. Irene didn't have a mortgage, she still lived in Aunt Diane's house. Angela had satellite service at both her house and Camille's house. She also fit the profile for someone who would buy $80 worth of chicken wings to share with the guests at her house as she sat around "The Roundtable" bad-mouthing everyone that came in and out her door.

Another theory I had was that the two of them worked together. Maybe Angela had the debit card and Irene had the checkbook, or vice versa. What I couldn't understand was how stupid could one of them be to write a bad check to themselves for $1500? Was it stupidity or was it just boldness? Whoever did it must have thought that no one was ever going to look into it.

I thought about what my mother had told me just days before. All of this must have been why I had really come to New Jersey, I thought. The insurance policy was just the sign that the universe used to point me in this direction. I had come all this way for all of this to be revealed and all of my feelings confirmed, once and for all.

After the dust settled on this investigation, I would no longer be able avoid the truth. I couldn't talk myself out of my gut feelings or try to downplay anyone's behavior.

I could be confident in knowing that I wasn't crazy all along. I wasn't hypersensitive. I wasn't delusional. Everything that my spirit told me was true. If I was right about this, I could be right about everything else. I had spent so many years talking myself out of thinking the worst about them, when they were actually worse than I had ever imagined. The feelings that I felt then would be confirmed also.

As we headed to the police station, the rain seemed to fall harder. The weather seemed to reflect my mood. I knew that I was crossing a line that I could never turn back from. I was reporting a crime, committed by a member of my family, that could possibly put them in serious trouble. I felt terrible about what I was doing but I wanted to know more than anything. A part of me wanted revenge but I know that having a vengeful spirit is of no use in this life. I had to evaluate what my true intentions were. Knowing was more important than the consequences for the thief. It wasn't about seeking revenge; I was seeking confirmation.

Because I sought confirmation so badly, any guilt that I felt about possibly hurting one of my aunts was overpowered. They had no regard for anything that I felt, so there was no reason for me to operate with any regard for them. Angela had just lost her job for stealing and told everyone how embarrassed she was by the entire ordeal. Apparently, she hadn't really learned anything from that experience. If she had the audacity to steal from her dead brother, then I could have the audacity to not feel bad for whatever would happen to her. We all knew Angela was greedy but I had never known she was this kind of a thief nor this greedy. The family was far from perfect, but we had some values.

The Woodbury Police Station reminded me of a Chinese take-out restaurant in the inner city. The lobby consisted of a walkup window with a door to an interrogation room that remained locked. The waiting section consisted of two chairs against a wall. You can tell that it's not a place for big activity. The town's biggest crimes include dogs barking too loudly, jay-walking, or harboring an unregistered vehicle in your yard. Reporting a fraud got me prompt and professional service. My report was filed very quickly and easily. The detective prompted me to give names of those who I suspected and took a copy of my father's death certificate. He assured me that I would receive a copy of the police report with details of the investigation in the mail.

On the way out, it started to sink in that this family feud was never going to end. It also sunk in that I was right about a lot more than I ever gave myself credit for. All of the making up that we had did before didn't mean anything. At the core, there was a lack of concern, consideration, and lack of love for me. There was no way that I could say that my family loved me after this. Love would have prevented them from abandoning me with a $13,000 funeral bill for my father, just to cause me to have to ask them for help. Love would have prevented Angela from emptying my father's bank account just days after he was buried. Love would have halted Angela from wishing me a nice life after I aired my grievances. The finality was devastating.

There was a reason why I had talked myself out of trusting so many of my feelings over the years. If I had trusted the cues from the universe, I would've realized many years ago that I was all by myself. If I had accepted what I knew to be true, deep down inside, I would have had to accept that my own family had always been my worst enemy. If I had accepted all of this years ago, I would have had to abandon the idea that someday I would have a loving, supporting, family unit. I didn't want to accept these things ever, nor at that moment did I, but I had to and I did.

I've heard it said that ignorance is bliss, and knowing is pain. I fully understand that now. I had always felt an emptiness, but could never explain why it persisted. I attributed it to my mother being absent physically and my father emotionally. I had always blamed them for my emptiness, but I had completely distorted the concept of emptiness. I wasn't empty because my parents weren't involved, that would've made me incomplete. Being incomplete pales in comparison to being empty. I was empty because not only was I lacking my parents, I was lacking a whole family.

How all of this was going to affect my relationship with Travis terrified me. I thought that I had worked through all my issues before I met him. Little did I know that the work I had done was nothing more than sweeping a mess under a rug. When I met him, my father's family and I were on good terms, and in a seemingly good place. I was very upfront with Travis about the history that we had but it seemed that we had moved past it.

Now, Travis and I found ourselves in the midst of a breakdown in my life. My father had died, my family abandoned me, and all the issues that I thought I had worked past were front and center and to the tenth power. I was scared to death. Travis was the only person that I had in the world. What if that was too much pressure? If I messed up things with him, then I would have no one in this world. Everybody needs somebody to love or someone who loves them. If he left for some reason, who would I have?

We overstayed in Woodbury, just as we had in Richmond, and ended up traveling again during rush hour. It took us an extra three hours to make it to D.C. with the traffic in Jersey, Maryland, and D.C. It seemed as if we spent the entire trip in traffic. On the way, I called my mother to notify her of all the juicy details of what we had uncovered. She sounded as if she was vindicated by the whole thing. For so many years, they had talked about her as if they were so upright and a little bit of her thought they were better than she was. My mother wasn't perfect, but she had values. To her, Angela actions were inexcusable.

Our time in D.C. flew by but we were still able to make some memories. The Martin Luther King Memorial was open and I hadn't been there since they completed it. Travis booked a really nice hotel room and we actually got to share a bit of romance. After touring, we had dinner and spent time not thinking about anything that had happened in the days prior. The rain followed us from Jersey and almost caught us while sightseeing at the Lincoln Monument. We barely evaded the ensuing violent thunderstorm by hunkering down in a not-so-memorable sushi restaurant in nearby Crystal City. It was a short-lived but much needed adventure.

Seeing D.C. helped me to check any negative emotions that I was holding onto from the disappointing day in Jersey. I psyched myself out by telling myself that I had simply took a trip to Washington, D.C.

We returned to Phoenix early the next morning. When we stepped out of the airport in Phoenix, we stepped back into sunlight and warm weather, a big difference from the cold and rainy weather back east. It had become a pattern to appreciate arriving back in Phoenix. The past few times that we had returned to Phoenix was after a crushing experience on the other side of the country. Phoenix had turned into home quicker than I could've imagined.

I made sure to tell Kyle about all that happened in Jersey. She was on the fence about whether it was Angela or Irene. She had such negative feelings toward Irene that she wanted to blame her, but she hadn't ruled out Angela. Kyle was still on good terms with Angela but that didn't stop her from saying that Angela should get in trouble if it turned out to be her. I really didn't want anyone to get in trouble but if it was Angela or Irene, they should at least be shamed, if nothing else.

I faxed the paperwork needed to get the $591 insurance benefit that had been left to my father by my great-aunt. I was still going to proceed with using that money to put towards building an empire. The check arrived a few days later and I opened a business account with the money. The deposit was symbolic to me. It was like my father and my Aunt Diane had given me my startup funds to go after my dream. Even though it wasn't as much as I would've imagined, I had to be grateful, and I was. The dollar amount didn't matter, there was a blessing on that money. The process of getting the money revealed a truth that had long eluded me. While the truth was devastating and hurtful, it was necessary for me to know to continue the healing process between my mother, my father, and myself.

CHAPTER FIFTEEN: HOW DOES IT END?

Just days after finding out about the insurance policy and returning to Phoenix, almost $6,000 was deposited into my bank account. I had long forgotten about my teaching job that I left in December, but they hadn't forgotten about me. My previous employer deposited three checks into my bank account with my full salary on each one. At the end of each year, teachers receive all of their salary for the summer months in the form of a lump sum at the end of June, the end of the fiscal year. I hadn't expected to receive such a payout because I hadn't been to work since December, but it came right on time.

I hadn't complained about or continued to even think about all that I had done to retrieve money from Aunt Diane's insurance policy. I just trusted that there was a reason behind it all and moved on. For that reason, I knew that I was being blessed. Nothing that was happening was a result of coincidence, it was GOD's favor. All the signs were telling me that I was headed in the right direction.

Two weeks later, I received a letter from the Woodbury Police Department. According to the police report, Angela had written bad checks to herself totaling nearly $3,000. The report listed a charge in the upper right hand corner written in a corresponding legal code. All of my suspicions that it was Angela who had stolen what was in my father's account were confirmed. More importantly, it was confirmed that Angela acted on behalf of her own best interest and definitely not mine.

My summer continued on and everything that happened moved further to the back of my memory. I continued to work my job and I started to write again. More than ever, I wanted to better my position in life and become financially independent of a job. I visualized all of the things that I wanted to do and have and felt a sense of urgency to complete my book. I could hardly wait to enjoy the fruits of my labor.

My career as a teacher was completely in the rear view and I decided that writing was how I was going to make a living. There was so much out there about struggling writers or writers who wrote part time, that sometimes I thought about failure. If I couldn't make a living as writer, would I be forced to go back into teaching?

Sometimes, I feared that I was wasting my time going after this dream but I would push myself past my thinking and continue to write. My book had to sell, I told myself. I had to be successful or I would have to go back to doing what I didn't want to do.

While I thought I was pushing myself, all that thinking began to make writing feel like a chore, and I struggled to continue. I was beginning to feel very tired from writing. One should be invigorated from doing something they loved. When you feel that love for what you are doing, that's when you know that you are in alignment with the universe. Some people refer to it as your calling. If I was making myself write, and it wasn't coming naturally, then I was working from the wrong energy source. I questioned whether I actually loved writing, or did I only love it because I had been lauded for it in the past?

All of these questions made it impossible for me to continue writing from a place of positivity, so I stopped again. It was another chance for me to work on being still. There was no need for me to answer my own questions. The answers I needed would come to me in time and at the right time. After struggling with stillness, being still had become easier than ever for me.

In the meantime, Travis and I set a date to be married. I had never intended on setting a date after all that we had been through recently, but it just came up one day. Travis' mother wanted to visit us in September, and he figured that we might as well get married when she came. There was no telling when she would fly out to come see us again, given she has a fear of flying. Just like that, we were going to be married on September 21st.

We decided on a Vegas wedding, so I expected it to just be me, him, and his mother. After all that happened, eloping was perfectly fine with me. The less people, the less negativity that we would have to worry about.

2016 was proving to be a year of extreme emotional highs and lows. In the midst of all that had been so upsetting, I had a love who would stick by me and continue to love me. All of the negativity that was surrounding me could've been my downfall, instead I continued to prosper. Just two years prior, I was alone, with what seemed like zero prospects of a relationship. I could barely get a date, or at least not with someone I wanted one from. Here I was, with a completely new life, planning to get married. It was all a reminder to me of how powerful we can be when we have both faith and vision.

July was spent planning our Vegas wedding and I avoided writing for most of the time. There were a few instances when I tried to write but I still wasn't ready. Every day that I wrote was followed by nightmares at night. The writing had conjured up my deepest and darkest feelings about my childhood and my father's family. They were like monsters to me, each one of them perfectly designed to cooperate with one another to inflict some sort of mental or emotional turmoil in my life. The nightmares were like watching my deepest and darkest feelings played out in a movie. I was in the same state that I was in when I first moved to St. Louis.

When I became a teacher, I learned about the various levels of trauma that children are subjected to. It was only then, that I was able to categorize what I had experienced. To be back in that space after so long and so much work made me feel even worse than it did the first time. How long would it take me this time to get past this? When and how would it end?

Planning the wedding was like drawing a line. If I excluded members of the family from my wedding that would signal the end, once and for all. If there was a reconciliation in the future, there was always going to be this memory that I hadn't invited them to my wedding. I still questioned myself as to whether I was oversensitive or flawed in my thinking. It was paramount for me to determine how I was going to navigate through my feelings in the future. Was I eventually going to forgive and forget or was I going to cut all ties for good?

I knew it wasn't necessarily fair to be upset with the **entire** family, but I had adopted a "not part of the solution, part of the problem" mentality. Everyone had allowed me to be mistreated and accepted it as the status quo. It was the same way I felt growing up. The only person in the family who was pushing back against my mistreatment was me. I was mad at everybody.

I had so much animosity towards my father's sisters, especially Angela, but Angela's daughters were my GOD-sisters and Etta's daughters were like sisters to me as well. Even though my cousins hadn't necessarily done anything to me, I didn't feel that anyone was going to bat for me either. Still, the idea that I was going to be completely cutting my family out of my life troubled me. No matter how bad people treat you or how bad a situation is, if it is what you are used to, it's difficult to just let it completely go.

I found some peace in realizing that I had been here before and made it through. And I didn't just make it through, I came out winning and shining. At age 17, the very same people threw me aside as if I was nothing. They abandoned me and waited on my failure. I struggled and hurt but I picked myself up by the bootstraps. Years later, when we mended our fences, I had an awesome career, a college education, and was more mentally stable than any of them. This time, I was in a better place to begin with. So, I would end up even better after the dust settled, except this time, I wouldn't be foolish enough to sweep anything under the rug. They would have to see how great I was from a distance.

By the end of July, I had come to a compromise with myself. I had bargained with myself about how I would approach inviting or not inviting family members to our wedding. I posted my wedding date and made a group on Facebook. I had deleted Etta and Irene, and Mya and I were never friends in the first place. Angela had blocked me after that heated phone exchange that we had. By posting it on Facebook, the news would get around that I was getting married but since they weren't my friends, they wouldn't know. It was petty and perfectly appropriate for how I felt at the time.

My sister saw my Facebook post and commented, "I wish I could come." I interpreted her comment to mean: I wish you would buy me a ticket so I could come. That wasn't happening. If it was important enough to her, she would make it a priority to find a way to get there.

After I prayed about what to do about my cousins, I decided to reach out to Camille and Shay, as well as Etta's daughter Tiffany. They were my friends on Facebook but I sent them a group text message, just to let them know that I was personally inviting them. I actually didn't expect them to come, but they couldn't say that I hadn't invited them. They were the last connections that I would have to the family.

Camille responded that she would get back to me. Shay and Tiffany didn't respond at all. Travis' mother made it clear that she wouldn't miss our wedding for the world, but other than her, I didn't anticipate anyone else making the trip out to Las Vegas. My mother quickly produced an excuse as to why she wouldn't be able to make it. I didn't bother to dig beneath the surface nor did I even care at that point. Besides my birth, she hadn't made it to any important life events and I had come to terms with it. After all of the progress that we had made, I decided not to take it personal. It was her issue, not mine. It was not my place to change my mother or make her be the mother that I want her to be. She is who she is and I am who I am. I was going to marry the person that I loved, and as long as he was there, I would be completely satisfied.

August rolled around and my birthday was soon approaching but I didn't really feel like celebrating. I had gotten much better but I still had a long way to go before I would feel like my old self again. I was proud of myself for remaining as positive as I had throughout it all, but I still recognized that I was missing a lot of my joy. Things were good though, just not where I wanted them to be. It was still going to take time.

While I couldn't bring myself to write, I remained creative by working on other projects. I worked on a *From Scratch* web-series, editing videos, and adding special effects. I was very proud of how much I had taught myself about video production within just a short amount of time. The video production was much more therapeutic and self-nurturing than the writing had become. I even thought that maybe that was what I should focus all of my energy on and forget about writing, at least for now. If I could barely write my story, who would want to read it?

A few days into August, just before my father's birthday, Etta called me in the middle of the night. Etta and my father shared August 7th as their birthday, born 9 years apart. She said that she was bothered by all that had taken place and it was looming over her mind, knowing that their birthday was coming up. It was the first time that anyone had called to discuss anything that had taken place.

Etta apologized for her behavior the night she tried to put Travis and I out, blaming her behavior on the situation itself. I accepted and immediately felt a sense of relief. I was relieved that my heart hadn't completely gone cold and that I was still able to forgive. I had worried that I would never be able to forgive and that I had developed hatred in my heart.

Her apology was just the opening for what turned into a six-hour conversation. We talked from late at night until the sun began to rise on both of our coasts. Etta lives in North Carolina, so that meant it was three hours later when she called and when we hung up. It was close to 6 in the morning Arizona time when we hung up. She had been drinking, but that was what I came to expect whenever Etta called.

I told Etta that she was the first person from the family I had spoken to. Surprisingly, she said that she hadn't spoken to anyone either, except for Mya. The two of them had some sort of bond that they had maintained since Mya lived with her doing her high school years. I never quite knew what caused them to be so close or her how that living arrangement ever came about.

Etta said that she went directly to her hotel after my father's funeral and then headed back to North Carolina. All this time, I had assumed that the three sisters had formed a united front. That wasn't the case at all.

The night of the funeral, Angela and Irene trashed Etta just as they trashed me. Again, proving that anyone who wasn't in the room became a topic of discussion. There was no loyalty, not amongst thieves, and Angela was definitely a thief. Lee's aunts not only told Lee what was said that night, but told Etta directly. The entire time that Angela and Irene called themselves bashing their sister, their friends were sending Etta text messages, in real time, as everything was said.

Angela made Etta out to be the bad guy of the entire family. Angela told Lee's aunts that Etta was the reason that I avoided the family during the funeral because of the altercation that we had. Not to miss an opportunity to be a victim, Angela also believed that she was owed an apology for the fight that she had with Etta that night. Irene just sat there and co-signed everything that Angela said.

Etta said that when she spoke to Mya, she confirmed it all but tried to throw Angela and Irene under the bus. Mya told Etta that she tried to tone down the rhetoric that night. That was a complete lie because I had been told everything that Mya had said. What I didn't know was that Etta had also been a topic of discussion that night.

Etta was most upset with Irene and even called her the fakest person she knows. She admitted that she expected more from Irene because they had grown very close. Etta also admitted that she expected this type of behavior from Angela, which spoke volumes to their relationship. They had always appeared to be close, even though they fought. Over the years, there were plenty of altercations between the two, but they always appeared to end up on good terms.

I was either 10 or 11, when I first witnessed Etta and Angela have a physical fight. I went with Angela to visit Etta in North Carolina, and somehow they ended up going to blows. I couldn't tell who was at fault but they were both out of control that night.

My grandmother lived with Etta at the time, but she took Angela's side without hesitation. It was obvious that my grandmother treated Angela as the favorite. Etta told Angela that she and her kids had to leave the house. That meant Angela had to pack up and drive 8 hours back to New Jersey.

The next morning, Angela packed up and headed back to New Jersey. Etta told me that I could stay, and so I did. It never crossed my mind that I had came with Angela, so I was supposed to leave with Angela. I wanted to stay and spend more time with Etta's daughters. I would only see Etta's daughters a few times throughout the year. My grandmother ignored me the entire time I stayed at Etta's, after she lambasted me for "getting in between sisters." As if it was my fault her daughters had a fight. Since I didn't side with the daughter that she favored, she actually accused me of trying to manipulate my aunts for my own personal gain. That was the kind of labeling and scapegoating I was subjected to growing up. I was a kid, just like any other kid, but I was talked to like I was sinister and calculated.

Etta and I talked at length about the longstanding issues within the family. She had never spoken to me so candidly before. Not only did Etta sound like she held resentment towards Angela but she resented my grandmother as well. She was also holding back years of disappointment and anger that she contained about the family.

Everyone seemed to have issues with the same two people, Angela and my grandmother. I imagined that this conversation we were having was the same kind of conversation that she used to have with my father. Since my father had passed, she must have felt comfortable enough with my level of life experience to share more of her life experiences.

Etta went on to make it very clear as to why she had such low expectations for Angela's behavior. Etta claimed that Angela only pretended to be close with their mother, so that she could get whatever she needed from her, basically saying that Angela used their mother. One story she shared was about a phone call where Angela begged Etta to keep their mother in North Carolina with her. Angela didn't want to be bothered with being responsible for taking my grandmother shopping or running her errands if she would've moved back to Jersey. I could understand Angela, in that regard, but my grandmother would've never believed anyone if they had told her that was how Angela felt.

The things that Etta said about Angela seemed like she had really been holding onto bad feelings for a long time. Etta thought it was unfair that Angela was allowed to use their mother's credit cards so freely. Even though both Angela and Etta's kids are adults, Etta was still bothered by times when her children wondered why Angela's children always got so many gifts for Christmas. Etta recalled Angela's living room filled with "gifts up to the ceiling," while her kids would just have a "normal Christmas," in her words. She wasn't jealous that they had more, she felt that it was unfair that her mother would help finance Christmas for Angela's children and didn't do as much for her children.

Etta couldn't make sense of it because she was a single mother after her divorce, and Angela has always been married. Not to mention, some of those Christmas mornings, my grandmother lived in Etta's house but still saw to it that Angela's daughters were taken care of all the way in New Jersey. Etta claimed that Angela ran up their mother's credit while she was alive and then ran up $40,000 in credit card bills in my grandmother's name after she passed away.

I believed Etta but took most of what she told me with a grain of salt. It was clearly evident that she had a deep-seeded issue with her little sister. When she started talking about my childhood was when I took the conversation to heart. Etta pointed out how wrongly she felt I was treated and how wrong she and everyone else was for allowing it to happen. She pointed out specific examples of when she was perplexed at how I was ordered around, cleaning the house, taking out the trash, and even keeping an eye on Shay as she used the bathroom. Shay was afraid to go in the bathroom by herself as a little girl, and monitoring her while she peed became just one of many duties, whenever I was at Angela's house. I had no problem doing chores as a boy, but I did much more than most kids, especially her own kids, which made it obvious that I was treated differently.

Etta probably had no clue how much her acknowledgement meant to me. She also had no clue that I battled to come to terms with the mistreatment in my childhood. I always felt it and knew that I hadn't imagined it but to hear someone acknowledge it, and also acknowledge that nobody did anything about it was important. That was part of the problem that I always had. Since it was only me who seemed to feel like something was wrong with the way that my family treated me, I thought I was crazy or oversensitive. Now that I knew that they all knew something was wrong, why didn't anyone do anything to help me?

Everything that Etta shared was both astonishing and confirming. I could not seem to stop the confirmation from coming. Etta was blunt, to say the least, about her mother and everyone in the family. To Etta, her mother was mean and damaged her as a person. I could definitely relate. My grandmother's words had damaged me and my father. She didn't explicitly state it, but she didn't seem to miss her mother. It was the very same feelings that I had wrestled with for so long. A combination of alcohol, resentment, and guilt had gotten to her, and it caused Etta to spill the beans.

Since we were on the subject of Angela and dishing so much dirt, I decided to tell Etta about all I had learned from my mission to New Jersey. My motive was to expose Angela and I wanted as many folks to know what she had done. I didn't want revenge but I didn't want her to just get away with it. There was no need to involve the courts because I wanted her tried in the court of public opinion. Etta salivated over the juicy gossip. She also seemed to be genuinely appalled and disappointed in her sister's behavior.

Hearing that Angela had wiped out and over

drafted my deceased father's bank account confirmed something for Etta as well that night. I wasn't the only one getting confirmation from this phone call. My father and Etta suspected that Angela pocketed money from an insurance policy that my grandmother had. She said they never told Irene about their suspicions, but they had been suspicious of Angela ever since their mother passed away.

When my grandmother lived with Etta, she always made Etta mail the premiums on her insurance policy every month. My grandmother would complain if she thought Etta was going to be late mailing it in.

One day, Etta noticed that she had stopped being hounded to mail in the premiums. When Etta asked my grandmother, she said that she had stopped paying them. It didn't make sense that someone would just stop paying a premium after paying for so many years. My grandmother claimed that she could no longer afford it, but she declined Etta's offer to pay for the premium. It didn't make any sense to Etta, and she suspected that Angela had taken over the payments and pocketed the money when their mother died.

After finding out that Angela lifted a few thousand dollars from my father's bank account, her theory about the insurance policy didn't seem as farfetched as it would have to me a few years back. I felt Angela was capable of anything at this point. I still thought that Etta may have been a bit resentful, which motivated her to believe her sister was that greedy.

Etta suspected that all of the trips that Angela had taken, a boat she purchased for her husband, and home renovations were evidence that she had come into some money from somewhere. When I thought about it, it made sense. The irony is, I thought that she had paid for that stuff with the money she was stealing from her job.

What if Etta and my father were right? I thought about a number of other things that had been brought to my attention. The evidence certainly pointed in that direction. I remembered being at the courthouse and noticing that an estate had been set up for my grandmother, and wondering what assets were listed. Maybe this phantom insurance policy that Etta was talking about was listed as an asset, just like they were going to do in my father's case, had it been worth some money.

CHAPTER SIXTEEN: BURNED BRIDGES

I turned 33 on August 14th, and I celebrated by spending the day at work. That had been the tradition for a very long time, so it didn't bring me any grief. I had given up on the idea of spending my birthday outside of work years ago. My birthday usually fell on one of the first days of school, if not the actual first day. There was no way that I could take off that early in the school year. It was a teacher rule of thumb. That didn't mean that I didn't celebrate my birthday. The celebration just had to wait a few days. That was exactly how things went this year also.

My birthday was on a Sunday and the following Tuesday, Travis and I headed to San Francisco to celebrate both of our birthdays. His birthday is on August 22nd. He shares his birthday with Angela while I share my birthday with his sister. When I first met him, I took it as a good sign that he shared the same birthday with my godmother and I shared a birthday with his sister. Now, he doesn't have to share the day with Angela, as she no longer has a place in my life.

We spent two days in San Francisco, and the time away was well worth it. The little moments that you have build up the momentum necessary to get you through to the next level. I needed all the moments that I could get to help me fully move past all of my frustration. Traveling always helped, and it was a perfect way to immediately take the focus away from negativity.

I appreciated the effort that Travis always put forth into trying to celebrate me and make me feel better. Even as I was taken by the bay and the wharf in San Francisco, I still wasn't as happy as I should have been. No matter how much I tried, I still had to keep working at getting my life back together. It was an uphill battle but I continued to fight. I was fighting for all that I had fought for before, but it was much more important this time. This time, I knew exactly what I was dealing with and what I was battling for.

Even though Etta and I worked out our differences, I made sure to impress upon her that we were having a very private wedding. She asked me the date and said she might have been able to make it. I told her not to worry about it. The way I said it though, was as if it would've been putting her out of her way to come, and I was trying to save her the hassle. It was actually my way of telling her not to bother. I forgave her, but that didn't mean I wanted to or needed to ever deal with her again. I was perfectly fine with leaving our last conversation as the last one we would ever have. We had ended that phone call on good terms and I was okay with quitting while we were ahead.

With the wedding date approaching, Travis and I started having issues that we never had before. They weren't serious issues, but it felt like my mind was playing tricks on me. I started to question whether he really loved me or if he pitied me. It felt like he didn't want to talk as much anymore and had withdrawn. He seemed to be negative and I was trying to get out of my negative space, so I could tell that he had moved into that same space with me. Little things started to turn into disagreements and arguments. We both had these attitudes, almost like we were tired of one another. There were a few times when I would just ask him, "Do you still love me?" He always assured me that he loved me, but we both seemed to be stuck in a negative space. He would blame it on work, or just day to day life, but he was acting different.

Up until that point, all of the time that we had been together was like a fairy tale and I loved him with all of my heart. I couldn't figure out what was making us both so negative in the month leading up to our nuptials. It made me nervous and extremely emotional.

All of the pressure that we had been under had

finally started to take a toll on the both of us. The moving, the starting over, the death of my father, the family nonsense, and now a wedding may have been too much for us to deal with during a span of nine months. I didn't want to lose him, especially now, he was all that I had.

This was not what I wanted for me and definitely not for Travis. More than ever, I had to refocus my thought process. I took to my computer and googled "laws of attraction," hoping to find some useful reading to help me. I found a series of YouTube videos that featured a woman by the name of Esther Hicks. Esther and her husband were the preeminent leaders of the new thought movement at one point in time.

When I first started learning of the laws of attraction, I watched the movie *The Secret*, and then read the book. It turned out that Esther Hicks was originally in *The Secret* film but had been removed. I started listening to Esther Hicks' teachings and while most of her teachings I had learned about in *The Secret* and *The Alchemist*, she delivered the information in a way that made it much more accessible for me this time. Listening to Esther, I developed a deeper, more practical understanding of the laws of attraction.

I shared the Esther Hicks' recordings with Travis, hoping that he would be open-minded to it. He was and he began sharing other recordings by Esther with me. Within days, we were sharing links back and forth via text message. Travis was putting Esther's lessons into his daily life and his demeanor shifted. I also tried everything that Esther suggested, and within a few days of listening to her lessons, I was inspired to write again.

After seeing how Travis responded to learning about the laws of attraction, I thought about how so many others could benefit from learning the concept. Sure, there were plenty of books out there by people who reached a lot of people, but what about one more. Maybe, my book could reach people like me and people who may never bother to pick up a book like *The Secret*, or *The Alchemist*. My story would definitely speak to a large audience, so why not help them at the same time. I know there are so many people out there who have felt the way that I've felt and lived a life similar to mine. I saw kids like me everyday as teacher, it was what called me to the profession.

So that was it for me, I had found my story and my inspiration. Esther said that when you are operating from the right energy space, what you do will feel good and feel easy. She was right. After that, I took to writing and it felt like I was doing something good for people. It wasn't draining or depressing, and it didn't feel like a chore. That's when I scrapped all that I had written about starting my life over from scratch, and started my story from scratch. The story of what took place during the time of my father's death was the story that needed to be told.

Because I was now telling my story with the intent to inspire, the words came and wouldn't stop. The writing happened so easily and organically. In no time, there was too much material for just one book. This story, is the first of many of my stories, that needs to be shared with the world. I had the foundation for an entire series, and this was only the beginning.

My days as a teacher were not over yet. I would teach people how they could make a better life for themselves, no matter how much they had gone through. My career as a teacher had not been in vain, nor were all of my years of education. All that preparation was preparing me for a much larger classroom, the world. With my writing, I could use all that happened in my life as a backdrop to deliver life-changing knowledge to people who were just like me.

A week before the wedding, I reached out again to my cousins just to see what the response would be. I was feeling better that Travis and I had moved into a positive space, thanks to Esther. I felt a little bad that I had lumped everyone in the family together as a common enemy. I knew that wasn't right, but it was so easy to do.

Talking to Etta reminded me that no one had ever had my back during all those moments when I was outnumbered and mistreated. Still, I felt that we had a bond of some sort and my cousins were just products of their environment. I called myself trying not to be judgmental, hoping that making small steps in the right direction would deliver me from any remaining negative energy towards my father's family. Simply put, I was trying. I didn't realize it at the time, but it was actually an act of forgiveness.

Camille let me know that she was going to be there. She must have talked Etta's daughter Tiffany into coming as well. Tiffany messaged me to tell me that she was going to catch a flight as well. I guess she needed some peer pressure, but she made it anyway. Camille also informed me that Shay wasn't going to make it because she was in school and studying for midterms. Shay didn't bother to send any communication on her own, which said a lot to me. She could have easily communicated that to me herself. Shay found time to post on Facebook at least five times per hour, every day. She could've found the time to let me know, if she deemed it as important.

Travis' mother, his cousin, and his mother's boyfriend flew in to join us at our wedding. Three of my best friends, including Brittany, bought tickets and booked hotel rooms just days after I announced our wedding date on Facebook. It showed me that people do what they want to do when they deem it important to them. I was so honored and blessed that they would make the effort to take off work and fly from all over America to meet us in Vegas for our special day.

We had guests come from Atlanta, New Jersey, Texas, St. Louis, Minnesota, and California to meet us in Las Vegas. We even had a wedding crasher, which I will tell you about in an entirely different book. Stay tuned for that story.

I hold no hard feelings toward anyone that didn't come. I just know that I hold a very special place in the hearts of those who did. Everyone who was supposed to be there, was there.

We stayed in Vegas for four days for our wedding and it couldn't have been more awesome. It was the first time in months that I felt like my old self. I was surrounded by my closest friends and people who were willing to go out of their way for our special day.

Our wedding was a spiritual experience that I can't begin to describe in words. It is a moment that I will never be able to appropriately write about because it transcends words and my own ability to communicate. When I think of the ceremony, I see it with a blur, like a dream sequence in a movie. I just remember feeling complete, holding Travis' hands, and staring into his eyes.

GOD made his presence known at our ceremony and he chose to speak through the officiant. We had never met this man in our lives, but he knew so much about us. He described our relationship down to the smallest detail, citing how our love grew out of being travel companions and friends. He also touched on the trials that we had been through and cited them as preparations for us to overcome anything in the future. He told us that love was about the little things that we do on a daily basis for one another.

"Do those things out of love and never out of obligation," was his advice to sustaining our friendship. That went deep. It was all that I needed to hear, and yet I never knew that I needed to hear it. It summed up all that I struggled with while coming to terms with my childhood. My family did things for me, but I never felt they were done out of love. They were done out of obligation. When the officiant spoke those words, it was once again the confirmation that I had been searching for.

All along, I felt there was a difference in the love that Travis and I had and the love that I had been told I had from my family. They always told me they loved me and would argue up and down that they just didn't know how to show it. Their proof of love was all that they had done for me, or that they were there for me in the absence of my parents. When in fact, they were part to blame for the absence of my parents.

The finality of marriage was initially terrifying. For so long, I wanted to be married. Up until the moment when we walked in the chapel, I hadn't had any reservations about it. Sitting in the waiting room before the ceremony, it hit me how final it was going to be. There was no turning back and my husband and I would be together until we left the earth.

The ceremony made me feel that we would be together beyond this earth, for eternity. GOD was there with us and HE was just as invested in our marriage as we were. I made a vow to GOD that I would love Travis, the same way that HE loved Travis. Marriage is serious business and I was going to have to put all that I had into it.

As soon as we got home from Vegas, I could tell I was already a completely different person. Getting married had categorized me into two people. There was a me before I was married and a me after I was married. Travis was so much more to me now. He was more than a boyfriend. He was even more than family. He was my husband.

I couldn't stop thinking about the ceremony and how I truly felt that GOD had entered into our vows with us. I never anticipated that it was going to be as deep as it turned out to be. Since I knew GOD was there that day, I surrendered all of my anxiety and nervousness to him. HE was in this with me.

The officiant's words replayed in my mind on a daily basis. Do things out of love and not out of obligation. Just a week after being married, Travis and I were both two very different people. We looked different, sounded different, even smelled different, all in a good way. I was so in love with this man that I would do anything for him. I always loved him before but now our love reached a new level. My marriage, in just a week, had become exactly what I had always wanted. We were more in love and more in tune than we were before. Marrying my husband felt like the rightest decision I had made, as well as the greatest blessing I had ever received.

The timing couldn't have been better. Having that direct interaction with GOD wiped the slate clean for me. I stopped thinking about all of the issues that plagued my mind for months before. Everything was exactly how it was supposed to be and I was accepting of all that had taken place. It was time to write, and time to share all of the lessons that I learned.

I had already finished the majority of what I thought was going to be my magnum opus. My problem was that I didn't know how I was going to end it. I had been writing and writing for months, and even re-writing, but I still didn't know how it was all going to come together. There was just a little bit more left to the story that I had to live.

After spending time with Camille and Tiffany at my wedding, I was grateful that they came out to support me. I was optimistic that it was going to be possible to cut my losses and keep them in my life. That got me to thinking about how I was going to maneuver in the future. If I was going to keep ties with Camille and Tiffany, it was inevitable that I would have contact with other family members. Camille was engaged, and would probably be married sometime in the near future. How was I going to support the people that I still valued in the family, yet keep a safe distance from the others.

There would always be some unfinished business. That was okay with me. I let go of trying to figure it out, it was in GOD's hands. I vowed to remain grateful for the people that I had.

Just when I thought I had figured it all out, I got a surprise phone call from Shay. At first, I didn't answer because I thought she had butt-dialed. I hadn't spoken to her since the day of my father's funeral, when Angela had her smuggle stolen funeral memorabilia to the car. That was six months ago and not a peep from her. The only communication we had may have been a like on Facebook. It was late at night where she was, so I couldn't imagine why she was calling. When she called back the second time, I answered.

It was just a few weeks after the wedding and I thought that she may have been calling to say "Congratulations!" She wasn't. She was calling to give me the ending to the book that I had been waiting on. It wasn't what we talked about that would be my ending, but the call would be the first event, in a series of events, that would lead me to the culmination of everything that I had learned, studied, and experienced.

It was almost midnight in New Jersey, which seemed like an awkward time to for her to call someone, unless it was an emergency. I guess it was an emergency to her, which says a lot about her priorities. Shay called to tell me that Mya had accused her of telling me about her affair with the married man. Yes, Mya and Shay were arguing about something that was said six months earlier. These people were like the gift that keeps on giving. The toxicity never ends.

At first, I thought that Shay wanted me to console her in her time of frustration. That wasn't the case. Shay wanted me to call Mya and vouch for her that she wasn't who told me about her relationship with a married man. That wasn't happening.

I was finally past it all and had no desire to go back. Mya was upset with Shay, because Shay was the **only** person that she had confided in. Angela told me, which meant that Shay must have told Angela, if Shay was the only person that Mya confided in. That meant Shay was actually guilty of what Mya was accusing her of. She just wanted me to get involved to say that she hadn't told me, but that didn't mean she had kept it a secret.

The next day, Shay sent me a text message lambasting me for not clearing her name. It was the audacity that I had grown so tired of. How could I have cleared her name, if her name wasn't clear? There was no consideration for me whatsoever. Shay then blocked me on her social media as well, the 2016 way of letting someone know they are cut off. It was fine by me. She had learned that from her family and acted accordingly. Shay was going to continue the generational curses and I was no longer interested in any of it.

For two seconds, I was irritated at the fact that these people just kept resurfacing with negativity each and every time that I thought I had finally gotten past it. My irritation subsided quickly. I was truly over it, once and for all. I was back to my old self again; the person I was before all of this happened. I knew that the altercation with Shay had happened for a reason. When GOD is working in your favor, even negativity, especially negativity, will end up benefitting you.

The next day, I did some cleaning and laundry, nothing special. As I was going around the house tying up loose ends, not thinking about much of anything, I decided to finally hang up the engraved wooden plaque that Brittany had given us for our wedding, as well as a painting we received as a wedding gift from a friend. I couldn't find any hooks to hang it up and I was thinking about putting it off again. Then I noticed a picture of Camille and Shay hanging on the wall. It was the perfect spot to hang Brittany's plaque for Travis and I, and the perfect opportunity to take down their picture. If Shay could dispose of me so easily, I could do the same.

It made perfect sense to remove the photo. I wasn't doing it simply out of pettiness, the action was symbolic. These people didn't belong in my home. Back in Jersey, I didn't see a single photograph of myself in Angela's house, Irene's house, or Camille's. So why were they hanging in my home? I took the picture frame down and headed upstairs to place it in a storage bin in our second bedroom closet. I contemplated throwing it in the garbage, but the universe had other plans.

The bottom of the storage bin was filled with pictures that I hadn't seen since I moved out of my own apartment and in with Travis. The pictures as well as most of the other items in the storage bin were from my single life and didn't seem appropriate for our life together. As I dug through the items in the bin to get to the bottom, a manila file folder caught my attention. The folder was labeled "goals" and I stopped digging to open it. Written in red marker on a sheet of lined paper was a detailed plan for the life that I wanted. It was written almost 3 years ago, when I had just started learning about the laws of attraction.

When I wrote it, I had made my mind up that I was going to have everything that I had ever dreamed of. I had discovered that my stubbornness could be used as an asset. On that paper, I listed all of the things that I was grateful for and all of the wonderful blessings that GOD had already given me. As it went on, I went into my wants, which included marriage and the freedom to explore my creativity.

All of those things had come to fruition, faster than I had ever expected. It all had worked. The people in *The Secret* had said it would work, and it actually worked! I manifested my wants into reality. I hadn't written that I wanted to lose my entire family, or even quit my job. What I had written was that I wanted to advance in my career and that I wanted healing from all that ever caused me pain.

Everything was the way that it was supposed to be. The family was gone because they obviously needed to be removed. GOD will make your enemies your footstool, and they were my footstools to help me step up to my next levels.

There was no logical explanation why I would've packed that envelope or how it would've survived two moves, one being across the country. I had written those goals before I ever met Travis, before I moved in with him, and even longer before I moved to Arizona.

As I placed the folder back into the bin, I noticed one of those large golden envelopes with a fastener. It was addressed to me at my old address in St. Louis, with my father's address listed as the return address. There was no postage on it, so it hadn't been mailed. I was curious to see what was inside. I had already been stunned by the goals folder, so I was ready for more. I opened the envelope and a greeting card fell to the floor. Then, I pulled out a thick packet of paper stapled together.

I saw my father's name and scanned over the front page. It was a $150,000 insurance policy dated September 3, 2009. There was a two-page welcome letter with his name and address and a policy number listed in the subject line. A page-by-page breakdown of coverage and costs followed. The breakdown was extensive, so I scanned through the pages quickly, looking for anything interesting.

Near the end of the policy was the beneficiary information. Angela was listed as the primary beneficiary, with Camille and Shay listed as secondary beneficiaries. The e-mail address listed was Angela's, from her old job. At first I thought it was the policy that he had refused to sign before, but then I noticed that the document was signed electronically, which meant that Angela had signed this policy for him, electronically, without his permission. My father had highlighted and underlined the date, amount, and type of policy, as if he was trying to scream something at me. I got the message; Angela had pocketed $150,000 from his death, in addition to the money she had stolen from his bank account.

Was I mad? Surprisingly not. The confirmation that I received was worth more than any amount of money that Angela received. I knew that GOD had way more in store for me, and what HE has for me, is for me. Angela would have to live with herself and her choices.

I opened the greeting card and found a picture of my mother and father on their wedding day. The card read: *Who would've ever thought that someone could make me smile as much as you have? Thank you for all that you've done and all that you are*. He highlighted the words *smile*, *you've done*, and *you are*. I felt like he was thanking me for burying him with dignity and acknowledging that he accepted me for the man that I was.

Underneath the greeting card text, he wrote: *I see and hear everything, drunk or sober, then smile, the best way to learn the HATERS....!* He was definitely trying to send me a message, and I got it completely.

All I could do was freeze. The moment was unbelievable. I'm sure my father gave me this envelope and card before and I just never opened it. That wasn't what made the moment unbelievable. What was unbelievable was the context, the timing, and the message that it sent to me. He was very much in communication with me, even if he had never intended to be. He was the angel that he promised he would be.

I felt more empowered than ever! I could finally confirm everything that I had ever felt in my life. What empowered me was that I was right all along, and I realized that GOD had blessed me with discernment from the day that I was born. I never should've ever doubted myself and I never will again. What an amazing realization!

The Alchemist came to mind once again. **SPOILER ALERT!** In *The Alchemist*, the boy traveled all over the world, looking for a treasure, only to find that it had been in the very spot where he first started his journey. The boy ended up back where he started and discovered what he had set out to look for. When the boy asked why he wasn't saved from all of his troubles, it was revealed to him that had he not gone searching for the treasure, he would've never seen all that he had seen, blessed all the people that he blessed, or learned how to follow the cues of the universe.

I had been on a journey throughout my whole life, just as the boy. I didn't search for treasure though, I searched for love to fill a void. The more that it eluded me, the more I worked to better myself and continued to live life. All that I had gone through pointed me in the direction of a treasure that had always been there.

Just like the boy in *The Alchemist*, my journey took me to places and to people that I would've never encountered had I not been searching for love. Nothing had been in vain. I made lifelong friends and impacted the lives of children. It was all part of the plan to get me here. Even a petty argument with Shay was designed in my favor. If she hadn't called me and started a petty argument, I wouldn't have removed her picture off my wall. If I hadn't put that picture away, I wouldn't have stumbled upon all the confirming artifacts that I had packed away years ago. This story was finished at that point, but it was also a new beginning for me, and the beginning of a new story.

My father's death was the hardest thing I ever had to deal with in my life, but in the process of dealing with his transition, I also transitioned from a worrier to a warrior through my own process of self-discovery. I learned who my parents really were and I was finally able to forgive both of them. I also learned never to doubt what GOD is telling you, even if it may seem farfetched.

Looking at the photo of my parents getting married, young and beautiful, my mother pregnant with me, I thought about myself as that little boy I used to be, scared, sad, and feeling unloved. He wanted to be a writer, but more importantly, he wanted to be loved. It took him a while, and it was quite a journey, but he had finally found the love that he had always been looking for. Along the way, he also had some pretty amazing stories to tell.

MORE TO COME

ABOUT THE AUTHOR

Before he ever stepped foot in Hollywood, Dennis Huffington had already mastered the art of reinvention. Early on in life, he realized that sometimes you need to just press reset and start over from scratch. His experiences growing up in a New Jersey small town and moving to St. Louis at the age of 17, made him wise beyond his years. That wisdom is reflected in his first book, *Inheritance*, which chronicles the converging of life lessons he learned in the wake of his father's death and the life lessons learned when he embarked on a journey to reinvent himself into a writer and media personality.

Writing on the book began in the early months of 2016 as a combination of memoirs and self-help principles. The death of his father during the writing inspired him to go bigger than he had planned. Originally titled *From Scratch,* Dennis realized that more than just one book was needed to deliver his message. The concept applied to multiple phases of his life, phases that many of us experience. Instead of titling the first book *From Scratch*, it became the name for a comprehensive series based on life lessons; lessons on love, friendship, spirituality, success, and failure. The first book in the *From Scratch* series, *Inheritance*, sets readers up for the complete chronicles of his life, which he believes have prepared him for greatness on his own terms.

CONNECT

JOIN MY MAILING LIST AT

WWW.DENNISHUFFINGTON.COM

FOR TOUR INFORMATION, UPDATES, AND EXCLUSIVES!

FACEBOOK.COM/DHUFFINGTONJR
@dhuffingtonjr

TWITTER.COM/DHUFFINGTONJR
@dhuffingtonjr

INSTAGRAM.COM/DENNISHUFFINGTON
@dennishuffington

DOWNLOAD THE FROM SCRATCH APP

WATCH THE WEBSERIES, PREVIEW BOOKS, CHAT, STAY UPDATED, & MORE!

BONUS CONTENT

EXCERPT TAKEN FROM FROM SCRATCH: BOOK TWO

NEMESIS

KINDLE EDITION AVAILABLE FOR DIGITAL DOWNLOAD ON

APRIL 11, 2017

As much as we humans try to control ourselves, we are a vengeful bunch. I know the bible says vengeance is the Lord's and I completely respect that. The bible does not say that vengeance is bad though, it's just the Lord's. To be clear, I am not seeking revenge but what better revenge would there be than to write a popular book about all of the things that I've seen and overcome. The names have been changed to protect the innocent. Me. I am the innocent. You all know who you are.

A major part of living is recognizing the times in life when there is a major shift or realignment. Some experiences and periods in time are before and after markers in our existence. Many of us distinguish what our life was like before and after we were married, had children, or some other major life event. If you're lucky enough, you won't have to experience a before and after event, whether positive or negative, until you are emotionally mature enough to process it.

When you are emotionally mature, you can come to a place of understanding and appreciation of the person you were on both sides of the before and after marker. Not only are you able to move past any negative emotions, but you will actually be able to see the value in what took place, regardless of whether the outcomes are positive or negative. Put simply, you will grow. That is, if you are emotionally mature.

Emotional maturity is not a given with age, it comes with living a variety of experiences that expose you to the growth process from which you learn and expand as a person. Experiences are neither positive or negative, but rather wanted or unwanted, desired or undesired. In the moment, they may evoke emotions that are either positive or negative, but the experience itself is necessary for us to be moved along our path. Experience develops our emotional maturity which later benefits our ability to use our emotions, therefore, strengthening our ability to harvest the power of our thoughts and emotions.

With emotional maturity, we become more courageous, less worried, and more positive in our thinking. Ultimately, we become better at utilizing the laws of attraction because we remain in a positive mind frame.

The contrast to emotional maturity is emotional immaturity, which also doesn't necessarily have a connection with age. However, it is more likely that an emotionally immature person is younger. We would hope that the younger you are, the less exposure to negative emotions you would have. Most of us want children to live in harmony and experience joy much more than the other negative emotions. With that being the goal, many children still end up experiencing more negative emotion than the positive.

So what happens when the negative emotion disproportionately outweighs the positive? The answer is: The lack of emotional diversity stifles the development of emotional maturity. The same goes for someone who has only experienced positive emotion. They will also remain emotionally immature. When something that prompts a negative emotion does manifest, they will be devastated and feel like it is the end of the world. It is only when the experience is over and they realize that the world did not come to an end that they can begin to develop their emotional maturity. When another similar experience arises, they are much better prepared to control their thoughts.

When we disproportionately have negative emotions, we struggle with a more detrimental form of emotional immaturity. Not only do we think the world is going to come to an end, but we have been waiting on it for a long time and may not even be frightened by it. A life with an overabundance of negative emotions makes it more difficult to have a positive reference point than it is for the person who has only experienced the positive. It becomes second nature for one to think negative thoughts, only furthering the manifestation of more negative experiences. It is a perfect and dangerous cycle.

Emotional immaturity is not a bad thing and one need not to seek out experiences that evoke certain emotions to develop their maturity. Life provides the experiences every day of our lives. To develop your emotional maturity, all you need to do is live. We should all seek happiness; the maturity will come naturally. Hence, the saying "You live, you learn."

When children develop emotional maturity too soon, it is often because they have been exposed to a diverse offering of experiences at a very young age. This can lead to children appearing to act older than they really are and seeking to satisfy emotional needs that they may be too young to have. Emotionally immature children, as many are, might not be able to handle challenging experiences appropriately. That's where adults come into the picture, as moderators and buffers for children who are still developing their emotional maturity.

The first before and after marker that I remember in my life was the day that I started middle school. I can see myself as two entirely different people before and after that day. I almost want to go as far to say that I had two completely different personal cores. My before core remained but in the years that followed, it was smothered and concealed by so many layers of negative emotions that who I was after I went to middle school would never be the same.

I didn't develop emotional maturity because I did not experience a single, solitary, positive emotion in the years that followed my entry into middle school. I only had negative experiences and I had them on a daily, hourly, and even minute by minute basis. It was HELL.

How I wish that I was exaggerating or using hyperbole to make this book more entertaining for you, but I am not. From the day that I entered the 6th grade, I entered a world of harassment, hatred, confusion, disloyalty, and anguish. It was all because of homophobia. My soul was robbed of everything that I ever had. I was diminished at every turn, and destroyed by constant disappointment and rejection.

I have prayed for peace, for even as a grown man, the scars run deep. Even as a grown man, I thirst for some form of justice, some taste of revenge. Not for me, but for the innocent me. I want retribution for the 11-year old me, the boy who was destroyed. Not for me now, but for the boy who dreamed of getting far away from it all; the boy who considered suicide. Not for the man that I am now, but for the man that I used to be; a man who struggled with his existence, believing the world was against him.

The only way I feel that I can help all of the boys and the man that I described is to tell their stories. They must not be hidden in shame any longer. They've been hurt tremendously and for me to continue to carry on the facade that they haven't been hurt, only continues to empower their transgressors. Instead, I will use their experiences to empower others like them, because they are everywhere, hiding in plain sight.

As I began to write this book, I thought of what I was truly trying to express. I wanted to send a message that would inspire, but the more that I relived my experiences, I was enraged just as if it had just happened yesterday. I was so angry and embarrassed that some of the people in my past were able to enrage me twenty years later. They still had power over a part of me. They were still my enemies. I was a grown man filled with the purest form of hatred for the 11-year old versions of the people I went to middle school with.

It was a big moment for me. There was work that needed to be done. As I wrote, I embraced the idea that GOD had made me special, and most people were put off by it. When you write about your own life, you can't avoid seeking understanding of your own experiences as you try to present it artistically. The more I explored the idea, the more it seemed like an effective angle. The only problem was that it began to upset me. I wasn't writing to make myself a victim but I was feeling like one. I couldn't get my message through, if I was still full of this hatred. I stopped writing and decided to let it rest until something happened. I didn't know what the something was but that's where the universe comes into play.

As I waited for GOD to show me my next steps, I began brainstorming some ideas for a title. The only thing I could think of at the time was *Nemesis* because it sounded cool to me and I was portraying everyone in the book as my enemy. I googled the term Nemesis, just to see how well it would fit. I wanted to see if there were additional meanings or literary uses. Most of the other uses were action movie titles or science fiction books that centered around two formidable, opposing forces going against one another, often for multiple sequels or an entire series. It seemed like my use maybe wasn't the most appropriate.

Being the scholar that I am, I dug deeper into the roots of the word. What I found was extraordinary. While I thought I was waiting on the universe to point me in the right direction, the universe had already sent me exactly where I needed to go. The definition of the term nemesis didn't fit my story too well but when I learned the story of the Greek Goddess *Nemesis*, I could barely contain my excitement. The story of my youth that I was writing directly paralleled the myth of *Nemesis*.

According to Greek mythology, Nemesis was a remorseless goddess who maintained an equilibrium amongst mankind. Nemesis measured out happiness and unhappiness and ensured that no one had too much of either. She has also been named *Invidia*, which meant jealousy and *Rivalitas*, which means jealous rival. *Nemesis* was seen as the personification of the resentment of people toward those who were blessed with countless gifts or good fortune.

It was exactly what my story was about up to that point. Of course, when I lived it, I felt so bad about myself that I was unable to recognize who I really was, let alone see the great talents and blessings that were bestowed upon me. The person I am now, who was writing the story saw my experiences much differently. I was rejected, not because I was less than those who rejected me, but because I was greater.

Remember, all experiences are neither positive nor negative, they all move us forward in the direction that we should be going, but the emotions associated with them can be negative. Trusting in the universe, I resigned to believe that *even* these tough experiences were part of a bigger plan, a clarity I waited 20 years for. If for nothing else, my experiences with bullying, homophobia, and suicidal thoughts would make an awesome book and could possibly save someone from contemplating killing themselves, someone else, or turning bitter as I did.

Enter Media
www.EnterMediaOnline.com